NUALA & HER SECRET WOLF

Drumshee Timeline Series
Book 1

From the reviews:

'... as a way of bringing a way of life long past vividly alive in the present, this slim little volume cannot be beaten.'
Books Ireland

'An excellent way to introduce history to
the eight plus age group.'
Dublin Echo

'The secrecy of the relationship, the incredibility of adults, and all the mystical elements of Iron Age Celtic culture are sure to be most especially appealing to the 8-10 year old audience at whom the book is aimed.'
Andersonstown News

*For the children of Inchovea School,
especially Edel Barry*

OTHER TITLES BY CORA HARRISON

Cora Harrison taught primary-school children in England for twenty-five years before moving to a small farm in Kilfenora, Co. Clare. The farm includes an Iron Age fort, with the remains of a small castle inside it, and the mysterious atmosphere of this ancient place gave Cora the idea for a series of historical novels tracing the survival of the ringfort through the centuries. *Nuala & her Secret Wolf* is Book 1 in the Drumshee Timeline Series.

NUALA
&
HER SECRET WOLF

Drumshee Timeline Series
Book 1

_____

Cora Harrison

WOLFHOUND PRESS
Celebrating 25 *Years*

Reprinted 2000
First published 1997 by
WOLFHOUND PRESS Ltd
68 Mountjoy Square
Dublin 1

©1997 Cora Harrison
Illustrations © Wolfhound Press

The Arts Council
An Chomhairle Ealaíon
Wolfhound Press receives financial assistance from The Arts Council/An Chomhairle Ealaíon, Dublin, Ireland.

British Library Cataloguing in Publication Data
A catalogue record for this book is available from the British Library.

ISBN 0-86327-585-0

10 9 8 7 6 5 4 3 2

Typesetting: Wolfhound Press
Cover illustration: Peter Gibson
Text illustrations: Orla Roche
Cover design: Sally Mills-Westley
Printed and bound by The Guernsey Press Co Ltd, Guernsey, Channel Islands

The wolf howled in the night. Again and again the cry rose up, and its echo bounced from hill to hill so that it sounded as if there were a whole pack out there, roaming the valley and surrounding the fort.

Nuala sat up in bed and shivered. She did not shiver from fear; Nuala feared no animal and the cry of the wolf filled her with a strange sort of excitement. She shivered because she was cold. She wanted to sit there and listen and imagine the wolf loping along the valley of the River Fergus, right up to the great forest of Kylemore; but her teeth were chattering, and she was forced to lie down again and wrap the sheepskin covering over her head and let her warm breath thaw out her icy hands. She could no longer hear the wolf. Soon the shivering stopped, and she fell asleep.

It was no warmer in the morning, though. Nuala had been very ill that year and, although she was better now, she always seemed to be cold – and this winter was colder than any other she could remember in her twelve years. The little round thatched house which she shared with her parents and her two brothers was bleak and chill on this February morning. She knew from experience that the main house in the centre of the enclosure, the house where they sometimes joined her grandparents and her uncles and aunts for feasts and special meals, would be even colder. The souterrain, where they stored the dried fruits and nuts from the autumn gathering, was always damp, and after a wet winter the heavy clay soil would be waterlogged and probably flooded.

No, there was nothing for it but to gather her courage and go out. It was no good huddling in front of a smoking fire any longer. The cold of the stone bench had begun to penetrate through the wolfskin on which Nuala sat, and she knew that she was not going to get any warmer by lingering. She got to her feet and, lifting the heavy sheepskin which hung in front of the door, walked out.

It was a windy day, although not as windy inside the fort as it was outside. Nuala went towards the entrance, her long black hair blowing over her shoulders as the gusty west wind penetrated the stone walls of the enclosure. She stood for a while gazing across the grey-green fields towards where smoke was rising from another fort on the hill opposite. Then she turned and walked around the steep sides of the fort until she faced into the strong west wind. She started running down the mossy wet fields to where she could see her father and brothers down in the flat fields which were called the Isle of Maain.

As Nuala approached, she could hear her father's voice raised in anger and the sound of heavy blows. Her brothers' voices were shrill and there was a note of fear in the voice of Niall, who was the younger of the two.

Climbing on top of the stone wall, she could see the reason for the fear: a large she-wolf had attacked one of the calves. The calf lay bleeding on the ground and fifteen-year-old Ciaran was endeavouring to stop the flow of blood with handfuls of moss. However, it was upon her father that her horrified gaze rested. She had never seen him like this before. She knew how important the cattle were to him; Usna would stay up all night with a cow who was giving birth. Nevertheless she hated him with all her might at this moment. In his hand he had a heavy club made from blackthorn, and with it he was beating the unfortunate wolf to death. In a moment, Nuala had run across the lane and was beside her father, clinging to his arm with all her strength and shouting.

'Stop, Father, stop!'

'Get away, you stupid girl,' grunted her father. With a jerk of his arm, he knocked her sprawling on the ground.

Sobbing helplessly, she watched him aim another few blows at the dying animal. When at last it was still, he went over to the calf, tenderly lifted her in his strong arms and examined her carefully.

'She may recover. I'll take her back to the house and we'll see what good nursing can do. Ciaran, take the spade and dig a hole to bury the wolf's body when we have skinned it. Then you and Niall go and search around – that wolf has been feeding cubs recently and there should be a den somewhere. Make sure you kill the cubs. We want no wolves here.'

With that he turned, ignoring his sobbing daughter, and strode up the lane carrying the injured calf in his arms. Nuala felt as if her heart would break. Never before had her father hurt her. Although he had often beaten the boys, she had always been his favourite and usually she had been able to influence him.

'Serves you right,' observed Ciaran, as he dug the yellow clay with his heavy iron spade. 'What did you expect Father to do?'

Nuala made no answer and presently Ciaran finished the job and went off with Niall. She lay there, wet, cold and miserable, and quite soon heard the excited shouts which she dreaded. Roused to new efforts, she jumped to her feet and ran as fast as she could down the track, until she came to an old quarry now full of briars.

The sight that met her eyes filled her with sick despair: the two boys with blood on their hands, even a smear on Ciaran's cheek, and at their feet four little bodies. She let out a wail of despair and Niall, who was feeling a little uneasy himself, relieved his feelings by shouting, 'Nuala's afraid of blood, Nuala's afraid of blood. Girls are stupid. Girls are stupid.'

Nuala turned away from them. Never, she thought, will I forget today. I will never forget the look on that dying wolf's face and I will never forget the sight of those dead babies. Still shivering, she walked back the way she had come.

I want my mother, she thought, as if she were once again a small child. Her legs dragged as she climbed the steep hill. It seemed years since she had run down it with the salt taste of the west wind on her lips. Once more she walked around the deep fosse, or ditch, which surrounded the fort of her clan, and entered the enclosure from the open eastern side.

Nuala's mother stood at the door of their house and watched her daughter slowly cross the large circular enclosure. Despite the fact that Nuala's face was pinched with cold and smeared with tears, her mother thought proudly and fondly that she was the prettiest girl in the neighbourhood. Her hair was long and hung below her waist in two glossy black plaits, her eyes were huge and dark, and already she moved with long-legged grace. She was dressed in a simple woven purple robe. The wool had been shorn from the sheep last year and then spun on the spindle, dyed with the blackberries which grew everywhere, and finally woven on the loom which stood in the corner of their house.

However, Eva's proud glance was tinged with anxiety; Nuala was not strong. Already she had lost three daughters, buried them outside the fort; was she doomed to lose a fourth? Nuala ate very little, shivered from one end of the winter to the other, was frequently ill and, as now, seemed to get upset over trifles more easily than any other child she had known.

'Come inside, my darling,' she said tenderly. 'You look cold. Come in and have some warm milk.'

Nuala came reluctantly and knelt in front of the smouldering peat fire, stretching out her thin hands to its smoky warmth. Her mother seated herself on the stone stool and gathered her daughter on to her lap, holding the mug of hot milk to her lips and petting her like a baby.

'You must not get yourself so upset,' Eva said softly. 'Your father had to kill the wolf. After all, she would have killed the calf, and soon there will be new lambs and we cannot risk them. What would we eat if we lost our animals?'

Nuala sobbed on quietly to herself. She knew that her mother was right, and yet something in her hated the thought that life was choked out of beautiful living creatures in order that her family should eat. As it was, Nuala made sure that she was nowhere near whenever the butchering was to be done. She sometimes suspected that Niall felt like she did but was ashamed to admit it.

'Is father still angry with me?' she asked finally, choking down her sobs.

'No.' Her mother's voice was soothing. 'He is sorry that you are upset and hopes he did not hurt you. You are lucky, you know. Most other fathers would have beaten their daughters for less. He knows how much you love animals. Come now, help me with the injured calf. See whether you can get it to suck some milk from your fingers. The poor thing has had a terrible fright.'

For the next hour Nuala helped her mother with the injured calf, feeding it, cleaning its wounds and bandaging its leg with strips of cloth padded with moss. The terrified look began to fade from the little animal's eyes, its breathing became steadier and it relaxed on the bed of rushes and soon fell asleep.

'There you are, now,' said her mother, 'there is no one like you for looking after sick animals. I think they trust you and they know how much you love them. You go out now and take a walk around, and see that the sheep have not been disturbed. They are down near the river.'

Nuala came out the fort entrance and hesitated. If she turned and went back in the western direction, she knew she would meet her father again. She could hear voices and guessed that he and the boys were probably skinning the wolf. Its warm fur would make a cloak for one of them, or perhaps a cosy bedcover. She did not mind the sight of the dead animal – she had seen many in her life – but she did not want to meet her father again for a little while, so she turned and went down the southern meadow until she reached the small river which flowed through the valley. In the summer it was quite low, but now it was in full flood and, as she looked into it, she caught a glimpse of the white underbelly of a fish.

Now she could see the sheep. They were wandering around in the far meadow, up near the Isle of Maain. Perhaps she had better go up and look at them more carefully, in case a dead or wounded sheep was lying on the grass behind some blackthorn bush. Slowly she made her way up there, already beginning to count off the sheep on her fingers in the way her father had taught her.

Two hands, she thought; there is one hand missing – oh, there they are.

Further up near the quarry she could see another little flock. She ran up and counted them off on the fingers of her left hand. Yes, they were all there.

Nuala hesitated. She could go home and tell her mother, but there was nothing to do. Her mother would only suggest that she sweep the stone floor of their house or that she cut some new rushes for the floor under the calf. She could, perhaps, walk back along the river and go to see the waterfall where she kept her small treasures behind a stone; or she could join her father and make her peace with him.

Nuala stood there; deep down, she knew what she really wanted to do. Fear, disgust and a morbid curiosity fought within her. The curiosity won and she continued steadily on to the quarry where the wolf cubs had been killed.

The sun had come out and it shone on the small bodies. Nuala stepped over them with a shudder and went into the den. She could see where the she-wolf had made a bed for her babies with pieces of heather, and she could see well-gnawed bones lying around. She was turning to go, half-blinded by her tears, when suddenly she stopped. The sun, now low in the sky, was shining directly into the den; and at the back, amongst the fallen stone, Nuala saw a flash of emerald. She was not alone.

CHAPTER TWO

For a moment Nuala wondered whether the mate of
the dead she-wolf was hiding at the back of the den,
and her heart almost stopped with fear. Almost at
once, she realised that whatever it was must be
something tiny enough to fit in between the boulders.
Holding her breath, she moved slowly and cautiously
towards the back of the little cave. She knew from
watching the wild hares and the pine martens that an
animal will often let you come quite close if it thinks
that you cannot see it, so, as she moved, she kept her
face turned away from the little creature. She silently
undid the iron pin which kept her cloak slung around
her shoulders. Step by step, she moved forward until
she was almost on top of the animal. With one quick
movement, Nuala dropped her cloak over it and then
reached down and picked up the small body.

The little wolf made no movement. Nuala expected
it to struggle or howl and certainly to do its best to
bite, but it did none of these things. In fact, the little
creature was very hungry and thirsty, but more than
that, it was paralysed with fear. It had heard the
shouting, the howls of its mother, and had seen its
litter-mates clubbed to death. During the cubs' six
short weeks of life, their mother had impressed on
them the necessity of staying hidden and quiet until
she had told them all was safe. Only this cub, the
strongest and cleverest of all the litter, had completely

absorbed the lesson, so now there was only one cub left.

Nuala cautiously undid the folds of her cloak and examined the cub. She could understand how her brothers had not seen him. His fluffy, baby-soft fur was jet black without a single light hair. If it had not been for that gleam of sunshine picking up the light from his eye, she would never have seen him.

Holding him carefully and firmly, she wrapped her cloak around her shoulders and tucked the little wolf under it, warming him with the heat of her body. She sat there holding him for some time and still there was no movement from the little body. She peeped inside the cloak; the wolf still watched her with fear in his gaze. Gently she stroked his fur and gradually she felt him relax. Presently his eyes closed and she knew that he was asleep. Perhaps he was dreaming that his mother's tongue was washing his coat. She hoped so.

As he slept, Nuala cautiously felt his body. He was thin, but not too thin. The wolf had been a good mother and had fed her cubs as well as she could. She noticed that he had a full set of sharp white baby teeth, so he would have been able to eat some meat as well as drinking milk from his mother.

Warm and cosy, the girl and the wolf cub sat for some time in the thin February sunshine. The sun had almost reached the west and soon it would go down. She had to make some decision about the cub. She did not want her father or brothers to find and kill the little animal, but she knew that it was too young to survive on its own. A slow death from starvation would be worse than a quick one at the hands of her father.

Perhaps she could manage to hide it and feed it until it was strong enough to survive in the wild. Then she could take it far away from their hillside so that it would never attack any of their animals.

As she sat there, a plan began to form in her mind. Her mother always complained of how little Nuala ate, so she would be delighted to see her take some extra food. She would be able to get some milk from one of the cows without anyone noticing. In the meantime, she must set about finding a safe place to keep the cub. She knew that it was quite likely that her brothers would come back to take the skins from the little dead bodies in order to make themselves some mittens. She got to her feet carefully and felt the little wolf lift his head. He made no noise and did not struggle, so she set out to explore.

As she looked around at the grazing animals, Nuala remembered that the High Meadow near the Big Meadow was to be kept for hay, so it was not going to be used for grazing. There was a rocky place where the bilberries grew in the autumn. She and Niall had found a small cave behind the oak tree there.

Keeping the cub well hidden under her cloak, she struggled across the rough ground, going in a wide circle in order to avoid her father and her brothers. On her way, she passed the black cow whose calf had been injured and saw with interest how full of milk she looked.

I'll ask my mother if I can milk her, Nuala thought. I can say I want to bring milk to the sick calf.

Soon she arrived at the High Meadow. She had remembered correctly. There was the little cave and, better still, there was a heavy flagstone lying near it.

If only she could manage to tip it over, she could place it between the oak tree and the entrance, and this would keep the wolf cub hidden for the moment.

Nuala hated to take the little animal out of the warmth of her cloak, but she had no choice. Like a wild animal herself, she was driven by fear. She quickly placed the cub at the back of the cave and stroked him gently.

'Stay there until I come back,' she whispered.

With all her strength she just managed to roll over the heavy flagstone. As she had hoped, it blocked the entrance and was kept well in place by the trunk of the oak tree.

'I won't be long,' she whispered. Then she turned and ran as fast as she could through the Big Meadow and up the lane towards the fort.

Twenty minutes later, she knelt beside the black cow and milked her into the wooden bowl which she had snatched from the stone dresser in the house. Her mother had been impressed by her thoughtfulness and had not noticed that Nuala had also taken a smaller bowl, one that her father had carved specially for her. Having filled the larger bowl, Nuala milked the cow into the smaller bowl.

'If I'm quick,' she said to herself, 'I will be able to give the milk to the cub before going back to the house.'

It was not so easy to get the cub to drink. He was deeply suspicious of the strange-smelling stuff and he had never before drunk from a bowl; he had only sucked his mother's warm milk. In desperation, Nuala dipped her fingers in the milk and, little by little, coaxed him to lick them. When his rough, hot little tongue started to lick between her fingers, she knew he was getting to like the taste. At last she was successful in getting him to drink from the bowl.

'You were a long time,' said her mother as Nuala came in with the milk.

'I know,' answered Nuala. 'I got a pain in my side and had to sit down and rest.'

Her mother's eyes clouded with anxiety; she remembered the winter when Nuala had had a pain in her side and everyone had expected her to die. However, as the evening meal was eaten, her spirits lifted: for the first time that she could remember, Nuala asked for a second slice of the meat.

The weather was warmer than it had been recently. Nuala was thankful for this, as she knew that the cub would be missing the warmth of his mother and his brothers and sisters. She wished she could see him again, but she knew that this would be too dangerous. The other members of the clan, her cousins and aunts and uncles, had just returned from their journey to the iron-makers, and all the men were outside in the fields trying out the new iron spades which they had bought.

'They make the metal by melting it out of lumps of iron ore in a very hot fire made from charcoal,' her uncle was explaining to her father, 'and then they beat the metal and they cool it in water. People say that too many trees are being cut down, but it makes wonderful spades and barbs for our arrows.'

Nuala knew that she would not be able to pass them without attracting notice, so she turned back to where the women were scraping the wolfskin. Her aunt had a new iron knife and was showing the others how much quicker it was than the stone knives. The women worked enthusiastically; it was not often that such a fine skin had been seen. An idea came into Nuala's head.

'Mother,' she said, 'could I have the old sheepskin which used to hang in front of the door? I should like to have it on my bed. I wouldn't be so cold then.'

'Surely, child,' said her mother absentmindedly. 'It is at the bottom of my bed but I do not need it.'

Nuala collected the shabby old sheepskin and tucked it under her bedcover. Her mother was unlikely to check whether it was still there, and tomorrow she would smuggle it down to the cave so the cub could lie on it. She slipped her hand under the rushes which lined her bed. Yes, the bread and meat which she had hidden earlier were still there. She slipped into bed and began to make plans.

Next morning Nuala was awake and dressed long before the rest of the family had begun to stir. She found the cowhide bag which she and her mother used for gathering fruits in the autumn, and cautiously, keeping a careful eye on the other sleepers, she slipped into it the old sheepskin and the food which she had saved from the evening before. Then she tiptoed to the door and hid the bag behind their house.

Having done this, Nuala poked the turf on the fire and added some more to it. When it was blazing up nicely, she went to the stone dresser which stood against one wall and took down a jar of oats and another jar of milk. She set the little three-legged iron pot, which was her mother's proudest possession, on top of the burning sods and carefully measured in the oats and milk.

When the porridge was ready, she filled a plate for herself and ate it thoughtfully. Normally she hated porridge, but now her mind was so full of ideas that she hardly tasted it. She quickly picked up the wooden bowl and, collecting the bag from behind the house, she slipped out the eastern fort entrance and went running across the fields.

As she ran, Nuala's mind was in turmoil. Could the poor baby wolf have survived the cold winter night without his mother to warm him? Was one small bowl of milk enough to keep him alive?

Almost sobbing at the thought of the cold, stiff little body which she might find, Nuala stopped by the black cow and quickly filled the wooden bowl. The cow gave her an indignant look as she ran off. She needed to have much more milk than that taken before her overflowing udder would be emptied.

However, Nuala was not too concerned with the cow; she would see to her later on. The immediate task was to feed and warm the wolf cub – that is, if he was still alive.

As she pulled back the heavy flagstone, her hands were trembling. For a moment, she feared the worst. The little wolf cub made no sound or movement. He had learnt the lesson of all wild animals: to stay absolutely still when danger threatens.

Nuala reached in and touched him and immediately her heart sang with joy. His soft fur was warmer than her hands and she could feel his little heart beating inside his ribs. Gently she lifted him out and placed him on her knee.

'You still don't trust me, do you?' she murmured.

Nuala held the cub on her knee and stroked him until she felt him relax and the hard thudding of his heart slowed down. Then she opened her bag and took out the food which she had saved for him. To her disappointment, he would not touch it. She had thought he would be very hungry, but perhaps he was still too frightened. She dipped her fingers in the milk and once more coaxed him, little by little, to suck until he ended by finishing the bowl. She tried the piece of meat again, but again he refused it.

Perhaps his mother chewed it first, she thought to herself, and placed the meat in her own mouth. When it was soft enough, she placed the piece in his mouth; and this time, to her delight, he chewed it and swallowed it. Bit by bit she managed to feed him all the food which she had brought. Then, quite suddenly, he fell asleep.

Nuala wrapped him up in the warm sheepskin and, placing him back in his little cave, she carefully blocked the entrance with the flagstone. Picking up the wooden bowl, she set off once more to milk the black cow. If anyone wondered why she had gone out so early in the morning, it would make a good excuse to say that she had gone to get milk for the calf.

As soon as the midday meal was over, Nuala stood up.

'Where are you off to, again?' questioned her mother.

'I'm looking for pretty stones for my necklace.'

Nuala's mother said no more. She was pleased to see her daughter outside so much these days, instead of huddled shivering over the fire.

Nuala went straight down to the cave and this time, to her delight, the little wolf cub came timidly towards her.

'Oh, you little darling,' she said, and stroked his soft baby fur. She fed him with the food that she had managed to hide from her last meal, and for the first time he ate hungrily.

How am I going to get food for him from now on? she thought to herself. I won't be able to hide food every day. Someone will get suspicious.

She did not worry too much. Something would turn up. Her clan was a rich one and never went short of food. So she sat there, happy and contented, with the little wolf snuggled into her, warm beneath her cloak.

Suddenly she grew still with terror. The sound of a heavy footstep was heard stumbling over the rocks.

'Ssst,' she said to the little wolf. It was something which she and Niall said to each other when they were hiding from adults. The little wolf stayed as still as a statue on her lap, as around the big oak tree came her father.

'What are you doing?' he said. 'I hope you are not catching cold.'

'I am just sitting down for a minute,' she said innocently. 'I've been climbing and I was out of breath.'

'Well, don't stay too long,' he warned. Soon, with his long strides, he was out of sight.

All that afternoon, Nuala played a game with her wolf cub. She ran here and there with him, tickled him, chased him, let him chase her – and then suddenly, without warning, she would hiss 'Ssst' and quickly cover him up and make him lie still until she told him to come out. She realised his only safety lay in making him understand that he had to hide and stay still when she told him to. It seemed as if the cub understood the seriousness of the game as well as she did, because by the end of the afternoon, he had completely mastered it.

When evening came, Nuala once again milked the black cow. This time the little wolf cub swallowed the milk hungrily and licked out the bowl. Nuala kissed him gently, put him back on his sheepskin, and went home, still puzzling over the problem of where to get food for her new friend.

CHAPTER THREE

Next morning, when Nuala had come back from seeing to the wolf cub, her mother was waiting for her at the door of their house.

'Nuala, I want you to go over to Mahon's place,' she said. 'I want to borrow a bag of sea salt, as I need to salt the fish which your father and the boys will catch. They have gone to the sea today, all of them except Ciaran, and they will be away for seven or ten days. Tell Orla that I will send her some salted fish in return.'

Fish, thought Nuala; that will be something to feed the cub.

Cheerfully she took up the bag and set off across the fields, going east to where the Mahon fort was, on the top of the next hill. She was pleased to be going, because Maeve, Mahon's and Orla's daughter, was the same age as herself and her best friend.

As she climbed the hill, Nuala pondered over her problem: should she tell Maeve about the wolf cub? On the one hand, there was the fear that Maeve might betray the secret. Perhaps she would be too frightened to keep quiet. After all, the very word 'wolf' was enough to strike fear into the heart of even the boldest member of the clan.

On the other hand, it would be very difficult to keep such a big secret from Maeve. Already she must be wondering what had kept her friend away from her during the past few days. Nuala knew her pleasure and excitement in the little cub would be doubled by sharing with her friend. It would also be easier for two to keep the secret, as one could be on guard while the other looked after the cub.

With her mind made up to trust Maeve, Nuala came in the eastern gate of the Mahon fort. It was less than half the size of their fort, just forty paces across, and only Maeve's family lived there. There was no underground storage chamber such as her family owned, and there was just the one house and a few cabins for the pigs. Maeve's mother Orla was just coming out of one of the cabins with the empty pig food basket. Nuala gave the message.

'Certainly, child, I will be happy to lend the salt,' said Orla. 'You go and find Maeve. She is milking the cow in the bottom pasture. I will get the salt ready and Maeve can go back with you and help you to carry the bag.'

Nuala skipped happily down the hill and burst upon her friend.

'Maeve,' she said, 'I have such a secret! You will never guess.'

Although Maeve was the same age as Nuala, she was much smaller. She had a halo of bright gold curls around her head, blue eyes, freckles and pink cheeks. She looked up at her friend, eyes wide with interest. Life was never dull while Nuala was around. Nuala had a wonderful imagination and her mind was full of all the old tales which Finn, her grandfather, had told her.

'What is it?' she asked.

'First you must swear that you will never tell anyone.'

Maeve promised readily.

Nuala told the whole story, beginning with the death of the she-wolf. Maeve was filled with amazement, tinged with terror.

'Your father will kill you if he finds out,' she said.

'No, he won't,' said Nuala, who knew her father better than Maeve did.

The two friends collected the bag of salt and, having deposited it in Nuala's house, they crossed over to the High Meadow and Nuala removed the flagstone and prepared to show her pet to her friend. To her surprise, no little black body appeared and for a moment Nuala was afraid that he had escaped or, worse still, had been discovered, but then she realised what the matter was.

'He is afraid of you,' she told Maeve. 'Just move away for a minute. He trusts me now and he will soon get used to you.'

After a few minutes of coaxing, the little black cub came out and sat on Nuala's knee and Maeve approached cautiously.

'Does he bite?' she asked anxiously.

'No, he just licks me.'

Maeve stroked his soft black fur.

'What big, fat paws he has,' she observed. 'What are you going to call him?'

Nuala had not thought of a name until this moment but an idea came instantly to her.

'I'll call him Fergus,' she said. 'After all, he was born just near the River Fergus.'

For the rest of that warm spring morning, Maeve and Nuala played with Fergus. Nuala showed Maeve how she could make the cub lie still and hide when she hissed 'ssst'. Then they practised: Maeve would go away and as she came back, making as much noise

as possible, Nuala would hiss and the little cub would slink, silent as a shadow, into the dimness of the cave. They also taught him his name. Maeve would hold him while Nuala went behind the bushes and softly called 'Fergus' and the little animal would come bounding through, eager to reach her. He now accepted Maeve, but Nuala was his love, his mother.

As they walked home, Nuala confided in Maeve her worries about feeding Fergus and her plan to use the fish when her father and brothers came home.

'They will have so much that a little will not be missed,' she said. 'The problem is that they won't be back for seven to ten days.'

'What about you and I fishing?' suggested Maeve. 'We could go down to the river every day and no one would know whether we caught anything or not.'

'I hate fishing,' said Nuala with a shudder. 'At least, I hate killing them after you catch them.'

'Oh, you don't need to worry about that,' said Maeve in an off-hand way. 'As long as we can catch them I'll do the killing. It's quite easy. You just bang their heads on a stone and it is all over in a second. Fish can't feel anyway.'

Nuala said nothing. She was doubtful, but she stifled her feelings of pity for the fish with the thought that Fergus would have to be fed. It would be even harder than usual for her to hide scraps if there were only herself and her mother and Ciaran at the table.

CHAPTER FOUR

Ciaran was bored; he was bored and angry. His father
had taken Niall with him on the fishing expedition
and he had been left behind to take care of his mother
and Nuala, and to keep an eye on the cows. There was
nothing to do with the cows at this time of the year.
The calves had all been born and the cows suckled
them and grazed the grass, which was now starting
to grow rapidly. He wandered down to the Isle of
Maain; nothing was happening there. He wondered
vaguely if he could find another wolf. At least that
would provide some excitement. He swung his
blackthorn club and looked appraisingly at the
muscles in his arms. Yes, he thought, I am sure I
would be strong enough to kill a wolf – a young one
anyway, he amended. However, nothing disturbed
the cows in their placid feeding, so he turned away
with a sigh and walked back up the hill towards the
fort.

His mother was there in the little garden on the
south side of the fort. Eva was weeding her patch of
herbs and vegetables and she looked hot.

'Oh, there you are, Ciaran,' she said with relief.
'Could you get a spade and help me with this? These
weeds have gone really deep.'

'I can't now, Mother,' said Ciaran hastily. 'I've got
to go and look at something. I promised Father to do
it every morning.'

Before his mother could say anything else, he turned and went quickly down the lane, as if he had been on the way to something when she had called him. What could he find to do, he wondered. He thought that he would go and check on the grass in the Big Meadow and in the High Meadow. The hay would be the next big task when the fishing was finished. He cheered up when he thought of it. His father had promised him that he could do some cutting of the hay this year and he would no longer have to be with the younger boys and the women racking and turning the cut grass.

The grass in the Big Meadow was growing splendidly, he thought. Already it was higher than it had been in April last year, and in the light breeze it blew into smooth ripples. He walked up the lane and looked across the stream at the High Meadow. The grass there was not quite so good, but it was growing well, also. He looked at it carefully and then frowned angrily. From the little bridge that spanned the stream, he could see a distinct track in the grass leading up towards the rocky cliff. What could have made that track, he wondered. It seemed too big to be a hare's track. It must be a fox. Now that would be something for him to do. He would set a trap in the hedge and catch the fox.

He went back to the fort. His mother looked up hopefully when he arrived, but he frowned at her.

'I'm too busy to help you now, Mother,' he said with an important air. 'There's been a fox tracking through the grass in the High Meadow. I must trap it. It will probably have its cubs out there at night chasing each other around, and the hay will be ruined in the summer.'

His mother sighed and he added in an exasperated voice, 'Why don't you get Nuala to help you? Doing the garden is women's work.'

'Oh, Nuala is out with Maeve,' Eva said. 'In any case, this work is too heavy for her. It's too heavy for me and Nuala isn't strong.'

'You make a baby out of her,' said Ciaran angrily. 'Anyway, I must do this trap.'

Ignoring his mother's disappointed face, he went into the fort and, pulling up the heavy stone flag, went down the steps into the souterrain. They kept everything there. It was a good storeroom and now, with spring sunlight flooding in, he could see perfectly. The great barrels stood on the floor; most of them were empty now, but soon they would start to fill them with stores of fish and grain and fruit and nuts, ready for the winter. On one of the walls there was a shelf, and Ciaran looked along this carefully. Yes, he was right. There was the loop of iron wire which his father had used before. It was strong wire, much stronger than the wire that the boys used to catch hares. He would make a good job of this trap and at least he would have something to show for the week's work. He felt in his pouch to make sure that his iron knife, his proudest possession, was safe. Then he went back up the steps and replaced the flagstone over the entrance.

This time he went out of the south-west exit from the fort, so that he would not have to meet his mother again. He could hear Nuala's voice and Maeve's as well. They were both down by the river, he guessed. Having a good time, he thought sourly, laughing and chatting just as they usually did. He walked down past the oats, keeping close to the edge and noticing

approvingly that the little plants were growing well.
They did not get a very good crop of oats from that
field, but they had enough for their daily pot of
porridge and the straw was useful for thatching the
houses.

When he reached the edge of the Rough Field, he
looked around him carefully. Yes, he thought, the fox
must come through here. He hadn't noticed the track
before, because the cows were grazing in this field
and the grass was short; but now that he looked, he
could see a faint track leading to the little bridge, and
beyond the bridge a clearer track leading to the rocky
cliff.

He went up to the bridge. He knew just where he
would place his trap. Some willows grew on either
side of the wooden bridge, almost obscuring its
entrance. He would place the snare between two of
the shoots and fasten it to the stout old tree trunks. It
would be visible by daylight, but at night the fox
would be unlikely to see it.

He worked busily. When the trap was completed,
he doused the wire with plenty of water from the
stream in order to wash his own scent off it. Foxes, his
grandfather had often told him, were the most
cunning and careful of all creatures. He would not
run any risk of scaring them off.

He wondered whether he should investigate the
rocky cliff in order to see whether they had a den
there, but he decided to leave it for the moment. The
foxes would be used to human footsteps in the Rough
Field – every day one or another of the family was
down there checking on the cattle – but nobody had
gone into the High Meadow for a month or so, as it
had been left for hay.

Ciaran looked up at the sun. It was high in the sky. Only midday. Another few hours at least before his dinner. He did not know what to do with himself. The less time he spent near the trap the better.

He decided to go and see what Nuala and Maeve were doing. He would go around by the Isle of Maain and creep up on them and have some fun annoying them. At least it would be something to do.

Nuala and Maeve were fishing when he peered through the thick hedge of blackthorn which ran along the south-western side of the river meadows. That surprised him. Nuala never liked fishing much. Niall was usually the one who spent long hours sitting patiently by the river. Maeve too had a fishing rod, he noticed.

'Oh, I've got another one!' Nuala's voice was high and excited.

'Quick, pull it in,' said Maeve. 'Here, give it to me. I don't mind killing them.'

Maeve quickly banged the fish on the rock and then took the hook out of its mouth. Nuala shuddered a little but took the fish. It was a nice big juicy-looking one, thought Ciaran, his mouth watering at the thought of it cooking over a peat fire. He was just about to stand up and demand the fishing rod so that he could catch a few fish himself, when Nuala said something which puzzled him.

'Well, that's three fish we have caught now,' she said triumphantly. 'I think if we can get another one as big as that one we should have enough for Fergus.'

Fergus, thought Ciaran; who on earth is Fergus? I have never heard of any Fergus around here. He started to think of all the families and kin-groups which lived around them, but he could not remember anyone called Fergus. Then Maeve said something which puzzled him even more.

'Nuala,' she said enquiringly, 'do you think we need to cook the fish for him?'

'Oh, no,' said Nuala confidently. 'I'm sure he would prefer them raw.'

Ciaran withdrew silently. He went around the Isle of Maain and then, out of sheer boredom, he went back to the fort and did some digging for his mother. All the time he was turning the puzzle over in his mind. He said nothing, however, until dinner time, when he looked around the table with mock disappointment and said, 'No fish? I thought we would have fish today. Maeve and Nuala had already caught three of them by midday.'

Nuala's mother looked at her in surprise. Nuala felt a feeling of panic in the pit of her stomach.

'We ate them,' she muttered, with her eyes fixed on her wooden platter. 'I'm sorry,' she added. 'I should have brought some home, but I was very hungry, so Maeve and I made a little fire and we cooked them and ate them.'

Nuala's mother beamed. 'That's all right,' she said lovingly. 'It's nice that you were hungry. You could do with a little more fat on your bones. Ciaran and I have plenty.'

'And what about Fergus?' asked Ciaran, annoyed at this reference to his heavy build. 'I hope you kept some for Fergus, and gave them to him raw, of course.'

Nuala turned white. She gulped. She did not know what to say. Her mother looked at her suspiciously.

'Who is Fergus?' she asked.

'It's just a game,' murmured Nuala, hoping desperately that her mother would believe her. 'It's just a game that Maeve and I made up. We pretend that the river is a real person.'

To her great relief, her mother laughed. Ciaran looked bitterly at Nuala. It seemed as if she could always get away with anything. Nothing she did was ever wrong.

He was still suspicious about this Fergus. Perhaps it was someone the girls had met at the feast at Bealtaine in the beginning of May. He decided he would try to keep an eye on them for the rest of the week. It would give him something to do.

Nuala could eat little for the meal. She did not dare hide food in case Ciaran noticed. However, her mother, for once, took no notice of her lack of appetite,

as she assumed that Nuala had already filled herself
with the fish that she and Maeve had caught.

As soon as the meal was over and the platters were
put away, Nuala got to her feet.

'Where are you off to now?' asked her mother.

'Maeve and I have planned to pick some flowers,'
said Nuala, taking down one of the light baskets made
from plaited rushes which hung on the wall.

'Would you like to come with me and Ciaran?'
asked her mother. 'We are going over to Donogh's
place.'

Nuala pretended to hesitate and then shook her
head. 'I'd better not,' she said. 'Maeve would be
disappointed. She found a place with some lovely
orchids, beautiful pure white ones, and we planned
to pick them.'

It did not take Ciaran long to harness the horse to
the heavy wooden cart, and then he and his mother
were off. Nuala ran down to the river. The fish were
still in the cool stony pool where she had hidden
them. She packed each one in leaves and hastily
plucked a few flowers to put on the top. From now
on, she must take the greatest possible care. She
wished Ciaran had gone with the others.

CHAPTER FIVE

Maeve was late. In despair, Nuala was about to go and feed Fergus by herself when her friend arrived, breathless and hot.

'I'm sorry,' she gasped. 'I had to do all sorts of things. I thought I would never get away.'

'Maeve,' said Nuala, 'something terrible has happened. Ciaran was listening to us talking and he heard us saying that the fish were for Fergus.'

'Oh no,' said Maeve in horror. 'Does your mother know?'

'I told her it was just a game that you and I had made up, that we were pretending that the river was a person, and that really we had cooked and eaten the fish ourselves.'

'Did she believe you?' Maeve's blue eyes were wide with apprehension.

'Yes, she did,' said Nuala, 'but for a minute I thought I was going to get sick, I was so frightened.'

Maeve looked at her enviously. 'You are really lucky, you know,' she said. 'Your father and mother always believe everything that you tell them. You have a great time. You're never expected to help much, either. My parents are always after me to do things. Still, I suppose I don't do as much as the boys or as Brigit. It's quite nice being the youngest of the family, isn't it?'

'Let's go down to Fergus,' said Nuala. 'Ciaran and my mother have gone to Donogh's place, so we should have a couple of hours to play with Fergus before they come back. In any case, you can always hear the cart from a long way off. It makes such a noise on the stones in the road.'

'I wonder will Fergus know me this time,' said Maeve as they crossed the Rough Field together.

'He'll probably –' Nuala began – and then stopped in amazement. At first, she could not think what was holding the branches of the willows together across the bridge; and then she realised what it was.

'It's a snare,' said Maeve at the same moment. Both girls looked at it with faces full of apprehension.

'It must be Ciaran,' said Maeve.

'Do you think that he suspects we have a wolf?' asked Nuala, her voice a choked whisper. She felt frozen with fear. She looked at Maeve appealingly.

'No, I don't,' said Maeve, shaking her head. 'People never lay snares like this for wolves. This is a fox's snare. He's probably just amusing himself, or else he thought the track that we made through the grass was a fox's track. Anyway, let's go and feed Fergus and then we can talk about it.'

Fergus knew Maeve this time, and he was delighted with the fish. He had begun to feel really hungry, and he gulped them down in a couple of mouthfuls and then lay down at Nuala's feet and wagged his tail. She bent over and stroked his fur. His eyes were fixed on her.

'He really loves you, doesn't he,' said Maeve.

'Well, I love him,' said Nuala. 'I just can't bear the thought of anything happening to him. What am I going to do about Ciaran? Even if he doesn't suspect anything about Fergus, he will still be hunting around here, looking for the fox's den.'

'Could you move Fergus anywhere else?' asked Maeve.

'I can't think of anywhere,' said Nuala miserably. 'I was very lucky to find this little cave. I don't think it is safe down at the Isle of Maain. That's where all his little brothers and sisters were killed and Ciaran might go hunting around there again.'

'This is such a good place, too,' said Maeve. 'No one would ever come here in the ordinary way, and there are all these furze bushes around and all the rocks. Even when they are cutting hay in the summer, they won't come near to Fergus's cave.'

Nuala was silent for a while. She picked up Fergus and held him on her lap, cuddling him into her and kissing his little forehead. A look of stern resolution came over her face and she turned to her friend. 'I'm going to talk to Ciaran tonight,' she said. 'I'm going to tell him that you and I are the ones who made the track through the grass, and that Father gave me permission to play here on the rocks. Ciaran is too scared of Father to question him; in any case, it will be a week until they are back. I'll tell Ciaran that I caught my leg in the snare and that it was lucky you were there, or else I would have fallen in the stream. I think we should take it away now, if we can undo it, and we'll bring it back to the fort with us.'

Maeve giggled. 'It might work,' she said. 'Let's go to a different place, back there by that big oak tree, well away from Fergus's cave, and we'll make a little house there with some of these big branches. We'll put heather and moss over them to make a roof. Then if Ciaran comes poking around again, he will see what we are doing here.'

It was such fun making the little house that Maeve and Nuala were sorry that they had not thought of doing something like that before. If they hadn't known that they were tricking Ciaran, they might have thought that they were too old for games like this, but now they were glad of the excuse. Fergus helped too, biting through the tough stems of the heather with his sharp little teeth and scraping away large clumps of moss and carrying them over in his mouth. It was amazing how quickly he picked up the idea, and Nuala only needed to say 'good boy' and he immediately knew that was what she wanted him to do. He watched her all the time, and she only had to say 'no' firmly for him to immediately stop what he was doing.

When it was time for them to go home, the little house had been roughly built. Nuala put Fergus back into his cave, and then went back across the bridge and deliberately thrust her foot into the noose of the snare. She pulled until it tightened enough to cause a thin red line around her ankle.

'There,' she said, 'that should be enough to frighten Ciaran away from doing this again.'

Maeve looked at her admiringly. That wire must really have hurt Nuala's leg. 'You are brave,' she said. 'I'd never have the courage to do that.'

'I'd die for Fergus,' said Nuala simply. 'Now you see if you can free me. Break as many branches as you like. Pull the wire again, it doesn't matter. We must make it look real. I must make Ciaran afraid to tell my father or mother in case he gets into trouble himself.'

Maeve made a good artistic job of freeing Nuala; by the time she had finished, it looked as if something had indeed burst out of a snare. Nuala rolled up the snare and put it in her pouch.

'Do you want me to come back with you?' asked Maeve.

Nuala thought for a moment and then shook her head. 'No,' she said, 'I think I might be better frightening Ciaran by myself. If you are with me, I might look at you and start to laugh.'

By the time Nuala got back to the fort, her mother and Ciaran were coming up the path.

'Were you all right by yourself, darling?' asked her mother, while Ciaran was taking the harness off the horse.

'Oh yes,' said Nuala. 'Maeve came over and we played in the little house we have in the rocks in the High Meadow.'

Out of the corner of her eye, she saw Ciaran give a slight start. When her mother had gone into the house, she lingered outside and took the snare from her pouch and showed it to him.

'Did you set this, Ciaran?' she asked accusingly.

He looked at her, his face dark with anger. 'Yes, I did,' he said roughly. 'You had no right to touch it. There's a fox around there. I saw his track through the grass.'

'That track was Maeve's and mine,' said Nuala impatiently. 'We cross over there every day. Father gave me permission to make a little playhouse in the rocks under the oak tree. And look what happened to me. I got caught by your snare.'

Nuala thrust her bare ankle out for him to see. She was glad to notice that the red line was as dark red as ever and was beginning to show signs of purple bruising. Ciaran was speechless.

'I think I'd better go and ask Mother for something to put on it,' said Nuala. 'It feels really painful.'

'Oh, don't do that,' said Ciaran in alarm. 'I'm sure it will be better by tomorrow.'

'Well, I'm going to,' said Nuala, taking courage from his obvious discomfort. 'And I'm going to tell her that you set it, unless –'

'Unless what?'

'Unless you promise to leave Maeve and me alone and to stop following us around.'

Ciaran recovered himself a little. 'I'm not likely to want to follow you around,' he said loftily. 'I've promised to help Donogh for the rest of the week. He is building a new cabin and he said he needs someone with good muscles to help him. But if you like, I promise.'

'Well, in that case, I'll promise to say nothing to Mother. Or to Father,' she added, with her eye on him, and was pleased to notice that he flinched slightly at the mention of their father. Ciaran never could get on with his father and he always seemed to be in trouble for one thing or another, these days.

The next morning, Ciaran was up early and was already harnessing the horse by the time Nuala came out to go and see Fergus. He had even done the milking already, which was a bit of a nuisance, as Nuala had hoped to take some of the black cow's milk for Fergus. Still, she could probably squeeze out some more. Ciaran was a poor milker; he was too impatient to strip out the last cupful. She had neatly managed to conceal a bowlful of porridge, so that would do for Fergus as well.

By the middle of the morning Maeve arrived.

'What did Ciaran do?' she asked as soon as she met Nuala.

'He was terrified,' said Nuala happily. 'He has promised not to follow us around, but we must be very careful all the same. We don't want any more frights like that. Come into the house and we'll see if my mother wants anything done before we go fishing.'

Nuala's mother, however, was only too pleased to see Nuala looking so well and actually wanting to be out of doors.

'No, you go off,' she said. 'I haven't too much to do at the moment with everyone away.'

'Would you like us to bring the fish back with us, or could we have a little meal outside like we did yesterday?' asked Maeve, her face bland and innocent.

Nuala's mother laughed. 'Have your little meal,' she said. 'I am not very fond of fish and Ciaran will be out for the day. Have this cake of bread to go with the fish, but be careful not to set fire to the grass. It has been so dry and warm recently and the grass is very dry.'

'We'll take care,' Nuala promised, taking her father's flint down from the little hole above the fireplace.

'Let's hope we catch plenty of fish,' she said as they made their way down to the river meadows. 'We had better cook one just in case she comes down, or watches to see if we light a fire.'

However, she need not have worried; the river was teeming with fish. They cooked and ate two of them and put the rest aside for Fergus. He was going to have a good feed tonight.

CHAPTER SIX

Every day for the next week, Nuala and Maeve went fishing. Surprisingly enough, they managed to catch something every day. The time never seemed long to them, because they were planning all the things they would teach Fergus. They decided that they would teach him to track, so every time they managed to catch something, Nuala went a little way off with the fish while Maeve released Fergus. In the beginning, he ran around, frantically looking for Nuala. However, quite soon he learned to put his nose to the ground and track her footsteps and receive not only the fish, but also lots of praise and hugs.

The two girls were enchanted with their living toy. They kept up the daily practice of making the alarm sound and ensuring that he instantly vanished – and it was well that they did.

One day, to their horror, they saw a man half-hidden in an ash tree on the edge of the lane. Nuala hissed, and Fergus melted like a dark shadow into the dimness of the cave.

'Who is it?' whispered Nuala.

'I don't know,' whispered back Maeve. 'I've never seen him before.'

The man stayed in the tree for a long time. He did not seem to be looking in their direction, apart from a few glances from time to time.

'Do you think that he saw Fergus?' said Nuala in a low tone.

'I don't think so,' replied Maeve softly. 'I think he
is a spy and he may be planning a raid on your fort.'

'He won't go away while we are looking in his
direction,' said Nuala. 'Let's move around the back of
the rocks and pretend that we are going away.'

'What about Fergus?' objected Maeve. 'He may
follow us.'

'He won't,' said Nuala confidently, and she hissed
sternly at the little wolf to warn him to stay hidden.

Fergus had no intention of moving. Like all
animals, he could smell fear and he knew that Nuala,
his mother substitute, was badly frightened.

The two girls got up carelessly and moved around
the rock, talking loudly to each other. Then they
turned. Cautiously, on their hands and knees, they
wriggled up to the top of the hillock and lay on the
grass. They saw the man climb down from the tree
and, with many glances from side to side, steal back
down the lane and along the road to Tullagh.

'What shall we do?' exclaimed Nuala.

'Let's run back and tell your uncle,' said Maeve. 'He
will know what to do.'

Without a thought for Fergus, the two girls turned
and ran down the Rough Field and up the lane
towards the fort.

Left to himself, Fergus obediently stayed hidden at
the back of his cave. He was a little puzzled. Nuala
always dragged the heavy flagstone across the
entrance whenever she left him, but this time she had
left it open. However, Nuala's training had been very
thorough, and she had told him to stay hidden. The
gentle March breeze blew into the cave, ruffling his
coat, which had now started to grow its adult hair.

The wind, blowing towards him, hid his scent from another wild creature which lived nearby.

Under an overgrown blackthorn bush by the side of the stream, a hare had its form. A few weeks before, she had given birth to a family of five young hares. Knowing the girls had gone, she had ventured to take her family out for a few minutes of playtime. She could not smell the wolf, because the east wind blew his scent away, but he could smell her and the young hares, and some instinctive feeling told him that here was food.

Fergus knew that he should not move. However, he was growing fast and he was always hungry. The fish and milk and scraps which Nuala brought him did take away his hunger, but they did not completely satisfy him. The smell of these little creatures reminded him of the meat which his mother used to bring him, and the saliva ran from his lips in a steady trickle as he thought how delicious they would taste.

Slowly and cautiously he edged forward, keeping himself flat on his tummy. The hare's ears pricked, she turned towards the cave. Fergus froze. The hare relaxed. Fergus edged forward again. He was now within a few feet of the opening to the cave, but still the hare neither saw nor smelt him. Then, like a coiled spring, Fergus exploded from within the cave.

If the hare had been by herself, Fergus could never have caught her. But she delayed, trying to save her babies, and with that inborn instinct which is in all wild creatures, he brought his teeth down on her neck and killed her instantly.

Back at the fort, Nuala had only just remembered Fergus. She had told her story, first to her mother and then to her uncle, and had then been summoned to tell it all over again to her grandfather. Angry and frightened voices were rising and falling around her when suddenly her face whitened. She looked across at Maeve and saw, by the flash of horror in her friend's eyes, that she also had remembered that the flagstone had not been put in place. The two children, slowly and as quietly as they could, edged out of the crowded house and ran quickly down the hill and across the field. They stopped with horror at the sight that met their eyes.

Outside the little cave, the new spring grass was stained with smears of blood, and on the rock some bits of grey fur lay torn and spotted with red. Nuala could not bear to look. Tears ran down her face and sobs choked her breath. She turned and started to stumble away. For a moment, she could hardly make

sense of the insistent words which Maeve was pouring into her ear.

'Nuala, it is not him. Nuala, listen to me. It is not Fergus!'

Nuala turned and looked into the cave. There lay a very happy Fergus, just finishing up the remains of the hare. He licked his fat paws, rubbed them around his face and strolled out of the cave, climbed onto Nuala's lap and instantly fell fast asleep.

'I love you,' Nuala told him tenderly. 'Don't ever give me a fright like that again.'

'Look how fat his tummy is,' said Maeve. 'I wonder whether we could find any more hares for him. I think the fish might not be quite enough for him.'

'Ciaran sets snares down by the bog,' said Nuala. 'He often catches hares in them. I could go out early

in the morning and rob them. I know how to set them up again. Ciaran will never know.'

Maeve was silent for a while. Then she said thoughtfully, 'I think that we should tell Niall about Fergus. I am sure that we could trust him and he would be a great help in getting food. He would like playing the tracking games with him too.' Secretly Maeve rather admired Nuala's handsome dark-haired brother and was anxious to see as much of him as possible. Nuala was not so keen, but after some argument, she agreed. She knew that Niall was gentle and kind with the farm animals, and she hoped that he would be equally so with Fergus.

Next day, Nuala's father and Niall returned from their fishing expedition. They rode up the lane on their strong horses with leather bags of newly caught fish slung over the horses' backs.

For the next few hours, everyone was busy packing the fish into barrels and sprinkling them with salt so that they would last for several months. Nuala and Niall were set to work making holes in the flat fish with bone needles and passing string through them, so that forty or fifty fish could be hung above the turf fire to smoke. Nuala particularly enjoyed doing this because she had decided that it would be easy to slip a fish off the line from time to time and bring it to Fergus.

She and Niall were sitting in the warm spring sunshine outside her house while all the rest of the family were down in the underground storeroom packing the fish. She could hear her mother telling the story of the stranger to her father, and the voices of her uncle and her grandfather interrupting from time to time.

'Niall,' she said in a low voice, 'can you keep a secret?'

'What sort of a secret?' asked Niall curiously. 'Is it something to do with the stranger that you and Maeve saw?'

'A little,' she replied, 'but you must promise never ever to tell anyone about it. If you tell anyone, I will kill myself, because it will mean the death of what I love most in the world.'

Niall turned and stared at her. He was used to Nuala. She did get very worked up about the smallest thing, but this sounded even more intense than usual.

'Very well,' he promised lightly.

'Swear,' said Nuala. 'Swear never to tell, swear by the sun god.'

Niall held up his hand. 'I swear by the sun god,' he said with due solemnity.

Nuala paused, drew a deep breath and turned a little pale.

'I have a baby wolf,' she said. 'I look after him every day and he does things I tell him to do and I love him very much.'

Her brother looked at her with a face as pale as her own. 'You must be mad,' he said. 'I can't keep a secret like that. Father would kill me.'

'You promised!' reminded Nuala in a low voice.

'I know,' said Niall uncomfortably.

They sat for a while in strained silence, mechanically continuing with their work. Eventually Niall said, 'Where is it?'

'Will you keep your promise?' questioned Nuala.

'Yes,' said Niall reluctantly.

'Swear.'

Niall stood up and held up his right hand. 'I swear by the sun god that I will tell no person the secret of the wolf.'

Nuala looked at him happily. She was pleased that Niall was going to be part of the secret. They had always been the best of friends, until the last year when Niall had seemed to want only to be with Ciaran.

'Wait until this catch of fish is stored,' she said. 'We should be able to slip away before sunset.'

As the brother and sister worked together, Nuala told him all about Fergus: how she looked after him, what she fed him on, and above all how clever the wolf cub was and how she had taught him to track her footsteps. Finally she told the story of the hare.

'We must get him used to our animals,' was Niall's reaction to that story. 'We can't have him killing our calves and lambs. Once he kills one of them, he will kill again and again, and then he would have to be killed himself.'

About an hour before sunset, almost all the fish were salted and stored in huge earthenware pots in the underground chamber in the centre of the fort. The remainder of the fish were strung on lines and hung in the big chimney to smoke in the fumes from the slow-burning peat.

'Niall and I are going to milk the black cow, Mother,' called Nuala. Without waiting for a reply, she seized the wooden bowl and went off, closely followed by Niall.

'Look what I've got,' he said, and held out an old leather belt which had once belonged to her father and was still too large to be used by any of his sons. 'I thought that it might be a good idea to fasten this around Fergus's neck, so we could take him out among the sheep and make him understand that he is not to touch them. If he is as clever as you tell me, we might be able to make him understand.'

For the rest of the afternoon Niall and Nuala took Fergus amongst the sheep at the Isle of Maain, while Maeve kept watch, ready to give the alarm if anyone else approached. Niall held the end of the leather belt in his hand and Nuala walked beside Fergus and hissed angrily at him every time he even looked at a sheep. She forced herself to be fierce, although she hated to see the hurt puzzlement on the little face, which still looked more like that of a little black bear than that of a wolf. She knew, however, that Niall was right. If Fergus ever killed one of their animals, there would be no mercy on him. He would be hunted down and killed.

By the end of the time, everyone was well pleased with Fergus. He walked among the sheep without even turning his head, and lay down flat on the ground every time Nuala told him to.

'Well done,' said Niall. 'Tomorrow we'll try with the cows.'

The next day, however, Nuala's father decided that he would go hunting. The salted meat in the souterrain was beginning to run low and the clan needed some fresh meat. The sky was full of clouds, but that did not deter him. Soon they were all ready with their spears and their bows, and their leather bags for carrying home the meat.

'We may be several days,' he said to his wife. 'It all depends on how good the hunting is.'

They had gone by the time Nuala had returned from seeing to Fergus. The rain had begun to fall and she knew that her mother would worry if she stayed out in it and would, perhaps, come to find her; so once she had given Fergus his milk and a fish, reluctantly she closed the entrance with its flagstone and returned to the fort. She was going to go back into her own house, when something about the way her grandfather, Finn, stood at his door, gazing wistfully after the hunting party, made her cross over to him and slip her hand in his.

'Are you sad that you are not going with them?' she asked.

Finn said nothing, so she tugged him gently by the hand.

'Come in and sit by the fire,' she coaxed. 'Tell me a story.'

Finn smiled down at her and allowed himself to be led back inside the big house, where her grandmother was busy combing wool with a comb made from a flat piece of bone.

Nuala and her grandfather sat by the fire in the centre of the room, he on his usual stool and she on a sheepskin at his feet. He sat gazing into the fire, and said quietly,

'Do you remember what I said to you a while ago when you were so upset about the sheep being butchered? Do you remember I told you that all living things must die and that death does not matter, as long as the life has been good? Well, I am trying to tell myself that now. I have had a good life, a fine life. I've had strong sons and now my grandchildren. I've had fat cattle and seen them increase. But now I'm getting old and I can no longer hunt, and perhaps the time will come soon for me to finish my life.'

Tears came into Nuala's eyes. She loved him so much that she could not bear to think of him dying. She put her arm around his legs and leaned her head against his knees. She didn't really know what she could say to comfort him. There was no doubt about it. He was getting old.

Still, there was one thing which her grandfather could do better than anyone else she had met in her whole life: he could tell marvellous tales.

'Tell me the story about the Golden Eagle,' she begged. To her relief, the sadness was wiped from his face, and he lifted his hand and began the familiar rhythmic chant.

It was a wonderful story, a story full of adventure and courage and high daring, and Nuala's mind was glowing with excitement by the time she left her grandparents' house and crossed over to her own house. She wished that she could go and see Fergus, but the rain was now falling in torrential showers and the sky was the colour of blackberries crushed in milk.

'Oh, there you are, Nuala,' said her mother, as she came in. 'It is a terrible day, so I think the best use of it would be to do some weaving. I want to make a new tunic for Niall.'

In the corner of the house was a large frame made from wood. It had two upright bars and a crossbar along the top. Nuala's mother tied many lengths of wool across the top bar, looped them around a second crossbar going across the middle of the loom, and then tied the ends through some stones with holes in them, so that the threads would hang straight. The wool had been dyed with some of the seaweed brought back after the fishing expedition and it was a reddish purple.

'Mother,' said Nuala, 'I have a good idea. Let's do the cross-weaving with a different colour. We could use the blackberry-dyed wool and it would give the tunic a very rich, royal look.' In her heart, she wanted to do something special for Niall to thank him for helping with Fergus.

'Well, I'm not sure,' said her mother doubtfully. 'It might look rather startling.'

'Let's try a few rows,' said Nuala. 'Then we will know how it looks.'

So they tried Nuala's idea and the effect was, as Nuala had predicted, very rich and quite different from any other tunic which was worn by the men around. Nuala began to enjoy the work, and she promised herself that when the tunic was finished she would embroider a design in saffron wool on the front.

After a couple of hours, Nuala's mother stopped.

'I think I will grind the oats for the evening meal, now,' she said. 'I am sure that they won't stay out all night, not in this weather. The rain is coming down in torrents now. They should never have gone on a day like this. I knew it would not clear.'

'I'll carry on with the weaving,' said Nuala, hastily. Grinding oats was a job that Nuala hated. In any case, she wanted to get the tunic finished as soon as possible. She pictured Niall's pleasure when he returned from the great forest of Kylemore. She kept her mind resolutely away from the picture of the actual killing and, although she was ashamed of herself, she knew that she was longing to taste fresh meat. She was sick of salt pork, sick of fish, and, in any case, if they did kill a large deer, there would be plenty of scraps left over for Fergus.

However, when the men returned, they were empty-handed. Apparently they had found the tracks of a deer and had followed them for hours. The boys had their bows and their iron-tipped arrows, and the men had their spears with the iron-tipped heads. They were all confident of killing the deer once they had caught up with it. But in the dense forest, with the tree trunks so near together, all of them had managed to miss their target; in fact, her father's precious iron spear was badly damaged, as it had lodged in the hard trunk of a blackthorn tree.

Soon afterwards, Nuala's grandfather came in to see how the hunt had gone. He was as disappointed as they to learn of their lack of success.

'I know what you need,' he declared. 'You need a good dog. Do you remember the people we met at the festival of Lughnasa last year? They had a dog the size

of a wolf. If you had a dog like that, you could catch many deer.'

Nuala's father only grunted; his disappointment was still heavy within him, but there was a glimmer of interest in his eyes. It was left to Ciaran, the practical one, to voice the difficulties.

'Sure, where would we be getting a dog?' he questioned. 'There are no dogs anywhere around here and if there were, they would probably be worth the price of a cow.'

Niall's eyes met Nuala's and she knew that the same thought had come into both their heads. Was there any way they could make their father believe that Fergus was a dog? They would have to work very hard at training him to ignore the cattle and sheep – or perhaps, if they could get Fergus to round up the cows and sheep without hurting them, this would save all the family a lot of work.

She busily passed the shuttle with its blackberry-coloured wool in and out of the red threads, but all the time her mind was full of plans. Fergus was very clever at tracking; if she could make him even better at this, then he would be able to track down a deer far more easily than even a skilled hunter like her father.

With all these exciting plans in her mind, Nuala's was the only cheerful face as they sat down to a meal of oatcakes and fish.

CHAPTER EIGHT

The next two months were the happiest in Nuala's whole life. As March winds were replaced by the soft warm days of April, and the pale primroses blossomed in the moss-lined ditches, and the shiny march marigolds glinted in the fields, the three children, Nuala, Maeve and Niall, spent as much time as they dared with Fergus. May came, and the wild orchids bloomed in the fields, and blackthorn trees filled the air with the scent of their blossom; and still the fine dry weather lasted. Fergus was growing so fast that it almost seemed as if he were bigger every day. His mind was growing as fast as his body, and few dogs could have matched him for ability.

He was extremely obedient, following closely at the heels of Niall and Nuala, always ready to flatten himself on the ground as soon as he heard a hiss. He was also learning to hunt for himself, capturing young hares and rats with an inborn cunning. Every day he had a lesson to teach him to walk among the animals; and eventually, when they were quite sure of him, Niall took the home-made leash off him and let him walk, first among the cattle, and then amongst the sheep.

One day early in June, all the family except Nuala went to help Maeve's father gather in the hay. Nuala had pretended to be unwell and so had been allowed to stay behind. She was sorry to miss the fun of haymaking, but she had a plan and for this plan she needed the fort to be empty.

Once the whole family had disappeared over the top of the hill, Nuala went to work. She released Fergus from his cave and, with him following obediently at her heels, she crossed the stream and walked up towards the meadow on the side of the hill opposite to the fort. On this hillside, there were two large stone circles where the cattle or sheep could be penned if danger threatened. Nuala went around to the west side of the circle and, using all her strength, rolled away some of the stones so as to leave a gap. When she had done this, she crossed back over the little wooden bridge to the Isle of Maain. Her heart was beating fast. What she intended doing might turn out to be a disaster and might betray Fergus, but she had to try.

Signalling to Fergus to stay by her side, she walked gently and softly towards the cattle, which were grazing peacefully on the lush grass. As she approached, they lifted their heads in alarm. She stopped; Fergus stopped too and, without being told, lay down. The cows began grazing again. Slowly and quietly, Nuala and Fergus came nearer and nearer. The black cow began to move; the others followed peacefully. Nearer and nearer they came towards the little stream. This would be the difficulty, Nuala knew. The cattle did not like crossing the stream and they would try to turn away.

The black cow came to the edge of the stream, and turned her head. Nuala signalled to Fergus. Quick as a flash, he raced around to the side of the cow. To her horror, he gave a low growl, and for one awful moment she feared that he would attack the cow.

However, the cow turned her head away and seemed to make up her mind that the bridge was less dangerous than the wolf. Slowly and carefully, she began to cross and the other cows followed her. Fergus, again without a command, almost as if he knew instinctively what to do, dropped flat on the grass and waited until all the cows were safely across. Then he followed Nuala over the stream.

Nuala's knees were weak with relief. For a moment, she had doubted Fergus, but no more.

Steadily, working together like a well-trained team, she and Fergus drove the cows up the hill. When they got to the entrance, Nuala signalled again to Fergus and he raced around to the other side. They had a little difficulty with the last cow, who suddenly and unaccountably tried to turn and run down the hill when she saw her herd imprisoned in the stone circle. However, Fergus dashed in front of her, once more giving the low growl, which this time did not alarm Nuala, and he managed to turn her around and get her back in front of the entrance. She meekly trotted in.

Nuala stood and looked at the herd. Her heart was bursting with pride and joy. She had often seen her brothers and her father do this and, on each occasion, it had taken them a whole afternoon.

A small flame of hope began to burn within her. If she could prove to her father how useful Fergus could be, perhaps she would be allowed to keep him. Her grandfather had told her that dogs had come from trained wolves long long ago, so why not again? She bent down and lovingly stroked the young wolf, kissing his little face, which was now lengthening out to a proper wolf muzzle, and rubbing the soft hair behind ears which were now almost erect.

'Good boy,' she murmured, 'clever boy.'

Fergus lay there in the hot June sun, luxuriating in her praise. If only he could be with Nuala all the time he would be blissfully happy. However, when he was with her, he could make sure that he pleased her as much as possible, and he knew that this afternoon he had pleased her very much. He snuggled into her and lay there almost drunk with happiness.

Nuala had almost dozed off, lying there in the sun with her arm around Fergus, when, for the third time that afternoon, she heard a low growl rumble through his chest. She stood up in alarm and, hissing to him to stay quiet and still, she scrambled up the earthen bank on the inside of the cattle ring and cautiously peeped over the top.

Down in the Isle of Maain was that very same man whom she and Maeve had seen before. With him was another man, and they both had ropes in their hands. They were gazing around them, looking puzzled, and suddenly Nuala understood: this man was a spy, and he and his friend had come to steal the fat cattle which he had seen that day in March. He had probably seen all the family set out with their scythes and the wooden hay rakes and had known that they would be gone all day.

For a moment, panic seized Nuala. What could she do? It was too far for her to run and get her father. The men would be gone, and the cattle too, by the time she got to the bottom of the hill.

And then her heartbeats slowed down. The men were gazing around them in a bewildered fashion, and Nuala realised what in her panic she had

overlooked: there were no cattle there to steal. There were no cattle because she and Fergus had very cleverly rounded them all up and they were now safely concealed in the cattle ring. Nuala began to laugh softly to herself. It was almost as if she had known what was going to happen.

The men stayed for a while, talking, and once or twice she was worried when she saw them glance up towards the cattle ring. However, they obviously decided that if the cattle were there, guards would have been left, so they climbed out of the field, furtively slunk back down the lane and turned back towards Tullagh.

Nuala was glad to see them go. She had heard about another tribe, who lived near the sea, where a girl of her age had been stolen and never seen again. She had confidence that Fergus would give his life to defend her, but, after all, he was not more than four months old and might not be strong enough to defeat two grown men.

Her big problem now was how to tell her father about the two men. The more she thought about it, the more complicated it became. She could not tell her father that the cattle had all been in the cattle ring, because that would mean betraying Fergus. Her father would know that she could not have done that by herself. And if she did not tell about the cattle ring, he would wonder why the men had stolen nothing. Worse still, he might track the men down and hear that there were no cattle there that afternoon.

Nuala lay in the sun for some time thinking about what was best to do. In the end, she decided on her usual course of action, which was to say nothing. She dared not risk letting her father know about Fergus yet, so the best thing would be to say nothing whatsoever.

Having taken that decision – a decision which later on she would deeply regret – she got to her feet, released the cows and put Fergus back in his little home.

'See you later!' she said affectionately.

She then crossed the Big Meadow and made her way up the hill to join the others at the haymaking.

'Oh, good,' exclaimed Maeve, when she arrived. 'Were you really ill? You don't look it. Your cheeks are as red as fire.'

'Come over to the far corner,' said Nuala in a low voice. 'I'll tell you all about it.'

While the two girls busily turned the hay with their wooden rakes, Nuala told Maeve all about her success with Fergus and how the two of them, by themselves, had managed to pen all the cows in the cattle ring. Maeve was thrilled to hear about Fergus's cleverness, but when Nuala came to the part of the story where the two men appeared, her face grew serious and her blue eyes were wide with fright.

'You must tell your father,' she insisted. 'What if they come back?'

'They won't come back,' said Nuala, but she sounded more confident than she felt. A little niggling doubt was at the back of her mind, but she pushed it away. The only thing which mattered to her at the moment was Fergus, and she was going to do everything in her power to make sure that he was safe.

For the next few hours, Nuala worked so hard that by the time the family arrived back to the fort, she was exhausted and covered with sweat.

'Never mind,' said her mother. 'I will make a nice hot bath for both of us.'

The men and boys were sent off to do the milking, and the big wooden tub was placed in front of the fire and filled with water from the well. Hot stones from around the fire were placed in the water until it was hot enough. Nuala loved to hear the hiss as the stones were put in and to smell the steam. She knelt in the warm water and rubbed herself all over with a cake of ashes which her mother had made by burning ferns and briars. When she was scrubbed all over, she rubbed hazelnut oil into her long dark hair and then lay back in the tub and rinsed herself with the soft, warm water. A bath was a great treat. She would remember this day for a very long time.

CHAPTER NINE

Another two months went by and still the secret of Fergus was kept. Every day Nuala and Maeve played with him, and Niall joined them whenever he could. Fergus was now about six months old and growing in body and in cleverness every day. He was no longer jet black and bear-like; he had become a slim silver-grey animal with a proud head, large upright ears and a bushy tail. He was strong and agile, with legs made muscular by running up and down the quarry, and he had an appetite like a horse. These days Nuala no longer shut him in during the day, as Fergus knew well that if anyone other than his three friends appeared he instantly had to hide himself.

Best of all, however, was his cleverness. It appeared to the children that Fergus could learn virtually anything. In truth he was a highly intelligent animal from a highly intelligent race, but his chief motivation was to please Nuala. If she tried to get him to do something which he did not understand, he would look intently at her with his head tilted to one side, one large ear turned towards her, as if he felt that if only he could hear her properly, he would understand. This expression of his always made Niall laugh, as it reminded him of their grandfather, who was now slightly deaf.

Sooner or later, however, Nuala always managed to make Fergus understand. Fergus loved their games together. He loved to search the long grass for things

which they had hidden; he loved to play hide and
seek, lying quietly beside Nuala or hunting
vigorously by her side; but what he enjoyed more
than anything else was tracking Nuala's footsteps.
No track was too difficult for him, no ground too wet,
no scent too old; he always found her, and when he
did his joy was immense.

Day after day the children discussed telling
Nuala's father about Fergus.

'After all,' Niall said one day, 'he did say that he would like a dog, and Fergus is very like a dog except that he is much cleverer.'

'No, he did not,' contradicted Nuala. 'It was Grandfather who said that he should get a dog.'

'Well, he usually agrees with Grandfather,' replied Niall. 'And Maeve agrees with me,' he added.

Nuala, however, was uneasy. Once her father was told, there would be no way back; either her father would accept Fergus or he would kill him the way he had killed Fergus's mother. The very thought of this happening brought a lump to Nuala's throat and hot tears to her eyes.

The three children walked slowly back to the fort, discussing the problem. Nuala wondered whether, perhaps, she should tell her mother and ask advice, but she dismissed the idea. Her mother would never take the responsibility of keeping such an important matter away from her father.

'Fergus is going to get too big for that cave soon,' warned Niall, 'and we are finding it hard enough to feed him at the moment. Once winter comes, he will be much bigger and there will be very few hares around and he will be hungry.'

Nuala stared at him with misery in her eyes. She was responsible for Fergus. She was the one who would have to make the decision. She had long ago abandoned her idea of setting Fergus free once he was able to fend for himself; he was far too attached to her for that. He would never go away from her. An idea suddenly came to her and she turned hesitantly to Niall.

'I wonder if I could tell Grandfather,' she said. 'He loves animals and he knows all about them. I think that I could make him understand that Fergus is not a threat to any of our cows or sheep. I could let him see Fergus walking among the animals and I might even be able to show him how Fergus can round them up. I could choose a day when all the men have gone hunting. If he liked Fergus, he would be able to talk to Father. Father would listen to him.'

Niall stared at her uneasily. Finn was always very stern and critical with the boys and Niall was never at ease in his presence. He did not see the side of Finn that Nuala knew.

'Perhaps we should wait,' he began, and then stopped as he saw Maeve put her finger to her lips.

'Hush!' she said softly. 'Your mother is coming.' Their mother was at the western entrance of the fort, her hand shielding her eyes against the evening sun, which was low in the sky.

'Don't be too late coming in, you two,' she called. 'We are all going to bed early tonight. Your father has decided to start cutting turf tomorrow and we will start off at sunrise.'

The clan owned a large stretch of bog a couple of miles west of the fort, and every year the families went to cut and dry the turf which kept the fires burning in the little houses. The turf was important for keeping the houses warm, and in this damp, cool climate the fires were kept burning almost the whole year round. Also the fire was needed for cooking and heating water. Cutting the turf and gathering large stacks of it was, therefore, a most important part of the year's work. Normally Nuala loved going to the bog, but this year she worried about Fergus being left alone all day.

'I think I will pretend to be ill,' she murmured to Maeve. 'I can't leave Fergus shut up from sunrise until dark.'

'Better not,' advised Maeve. 'Your mother will be getting suspicious, especially as you are never ill these days. Don't worry about Fergus. I will go in the morning and again in the middle of the afternoon.'

Nuala thanked her friend and, parting from her, went through the gate into the fort. Her father, grandfather and uncle were sharpening the iron spades, called *slans*, with which they would cut the turf, while her mother and aunt were down in the souterrain getting out the big baskets, woven from the willows which grew beside the river. Some of the turf had been cut a few weeks ago and might be dry enough to be taken back, but the pieces which would be cut tomorrow would have to be stacked for several weeks to dry in the sun.

Niall joined the men while Nuala went into the house and started to get food ready to be packed in smaller baskets. They would probably have three meals while they were in the bog, and everyone would be hungry and thirsty after working hard in the fresh air. In spite of her worries about Fergus, Nuala was beginning to feel quite excited about going to the bog. She did not often get a chance to go on a journey or to see new places.

CHAPTER TEN

The sky was barely pink next morning when Nuala dragged herself from her bed. Everyone stood around blinking sleepily while the boys caught the strongest horse from the field behind the fort and hung the baskets on either side of him. There was a damp chill in the air and Nuala shivered. She did not think it was going to be as warm and sunny as it had been, but her mother was optimistic and said that it would clear to be a beautiful day.

At first it seemed as if her mother was right; the morning was fine and dry. A light west wind blew in from the sea, the birds sang and beautiful butterflies flew from flower to flower. The three men were cutting the turf and throwing the still-soft lumps up on to the bank, where the others were stacking the turf so that it would dry in the wind and the sunshine. It was hard work, picking up two wet lumps, propping them up against each other, then placing two more lumps on the other sides and one across the top so that it looked like a little house. After a few hours Nuala's back and shoulders began to ache, and she was glad when her mother said they would sit down to have their first meal.

Nuala had not as great an appetite as the rest of her family, so when she had had enough to eat she wandered off. She loved the bog, the little pools of brown water, the small white flowers whose heads were like wisps of cotton wool, and above all the many strange birds. Nuala wandered here and there, with her hand shading her eyes from the sun, trying to make out their colours and shapes.

Soon, to her excitement, she saw a beautiful golden eagle. She could see him clearly because the sun had gone behind the clouds. He was hovering over a dip in the bog about half a mile away. Nuala could see some gorse bushes growing there; the golden colour stood out against the chocolate brown of the bog. Perhaps he and his mate had a nest there among the bushes, thought Nuala to herself. An overwhelming desire seized her to see the baby eagles; she had never seen a baby eagle, although her grandfather had told her many stories about eagles.

As Nuala stumbled along over the bog, tripping over concealed roots of heather and splashing into puddles, her imagination was working at great speed. Perhaps she might find a baby eagle which had fallen out of the nest, and she could bring it home and tame it and teach it to obey her in the way that she had taught Fergus. Niall would make her a box to keep it in and she would bring it food every day until it learned to fly. Even after it learned to fly, she would still give it food so that it would always return to her no matter how far it went.

Nuala's mind was so full of the picture of herself striding the hills with a handsome, fully-grown wolf at her heels and a beautiful golden eagle sitting on her outstretched arm, that she failed to notice that the day had got cloudier and cloudier and a soft mist had begun to fall. She could still see the gorse bushes and she kept her face resolutely turned towards them, although the way seemed much further than she had thought at first. She was now on a section of bog that had not been touched for a long time. Finn had told her that it had been used when he was a little boy, but now most of the turf had been taken from this section and there were no other families anywhere near.

The day became worse; the rain was driving so hard in Nuala's face that she could hardly see. In fact, the gorse bushes were now completely hidden by a sheet of grey mist. Nuala kept going doggedly ahead. She knew that the gorse-filled hollow was to the west, so she reasoned to herself that if she kept the wind in her face, she must be going the right way.

Unfortunately, the wind seemed to be decreasing in strength and there were so many clumps of heather to go around and pools to avoid that Nuala was no longer quite certain that she was going the right way. She stood still for a moment and listened. She could no longer hear the voices of her family, but overhead, quite near to where she stood, she heard the crack of large wings beating, as the golden eagle flew slowly overhead.

For a minute Nuala was a little afraid. She knew that an eagle would take a new-born lamb. She had never seen this, but her father had described how it would land on top of the lamb, seize it in its huge talons and carry it away to its nest. Nuala never allowed herself to be afraid of creatures so, after a moment's hesitation, she resolutely pressed ahead.

The mist was getting worse every minute and there was now a thick blanket of fog around Nuala. She began to grow quite frightened, stopping every few minutes to listen, straining to hear if there were any sounds of voices in the distance. She realised that she had been foolish to keep going once the heavy rain had begun to fall. She should have known how rapidly these mists blew in from the ocean and how they could stay for days.

There was no point in going on; in any case, she would not be able to see anything in this mist. She would have to turn back.

Nuala turned around and started to make her way back. The fog was now so thick that she could hardly see her hand in front of her eyes. She felt a clump of heather in front of her and stepped over it, only to find that she had stepped onto empty space and that she was falling, helplessly, over the side of a steep cliff.

She had fallen over the edge of a sheer cliff, a place where, in the past, slabs of stone had been hacked out in order to build houses and forts. It was a long time since the quarry had been used, and plants and bushes had grown over the steep sides. As she fell, Nuala had the presence of mind to snatch at a branch from one of the bushes. The branch broke, but it slowed her fall. Down, down she fell – now painfully scraping against exposed slabs of stone, now tearing her hands on the great hooked thorns of the briars – until, bruised and bleeding, she landed at the bottom of the precipice.

Nuala lay there for some time. She could feel that her face was wet, and from its stickiness she realised that she was bleeding profusely from a cut on her forehead. She found it hard to care much. She had struck her head several times on the way down and now had a dreamy, unreal feeling. There was a loud singing noise in her ears and her whole body was drenched in sweat. Although she did not know it, she was fast losing consciousness. Her eyes closed and her head sank down on the hard stone.

She was aroused by a harsh screech; the eagle had come back, and although the heavy fog prevented her seeing him, she could hear the creak of the huge wings overhead. Struggling through the mists of unconsciousness, Nuala became aware of the danger she was in. There was no doubt that the eagle was likely to attack her, as she must now be near its nest. Somehow she must gather her strength and get away from here.

Sick and dizzy, she tried to get to her feet, only to sink down again with a cry of pain. She was unable to stand. During her fall she must have broken her leg. There was no possibility of escape from the quarry.

'Never mind,' she thought to herself. 'They'll find me. I know that my father will keep looking and never give up until he finds me.'

Her courage began to return and she looked around her to see if there was anything she could use to keep her safe until she was found. Not far from where she was lying, she could see a young bush. As she fell she must have grabbed hold of it and pulled it down with her. Inch by inch she struggled along the ground towards it. Her broken leg sent such waves of agony through her that she could feel the sweat running down her face and could taste its salt on her lips.

She stopped to rest, sobbing quietly under her breath. The bush was only a few feet away, but the pain from her broken leg was so intense that it took more courage than she had ever needed in her life for her to start again the slow and painful edging forward.

Nearer and nearer she came. Her hand just touched the small trunk. She was a few inches too far away to get a secure grip.

She moved forward again, but by an evil fate, her shoulder was resting on some loose stones. She slipped, and the bush rolled away and came to rest about twelve feet below her. It was too much; for the second time Nuala fainted.

When Nuala came back to consciousness this time, her leg was mercifully numb. She made no further effort to reach the bush. She was only thankful not to have to experience the searing agony of her broken bones. In any case, she could no longer hear the eagle circling overhead. Perhaps he had not been able to see her in the fog, or perhaps he had realised that she was no threat to his young and too big to provide a meal.

However, a new worry came to mind. There was still a heavy mist falling and she was soaked to the skin. Uncontrollable shivers shook her body and she was colder than she had ever been in her life. Even though she could see very little around her, Nuala instinctively knew that it was beginning to get darker. Soon it would be the longest day of the year, so she must have been unconscious for many hours.

Hope now began to fade. Nuala had very little idea of how far she had gone from her family, and she guessed that they had not taken much notice of her as she wandered off. They might even have passed quite near her while she was unconscious and unable to hear them. She sobbed quietly to herself as she lay on the cold wet ground.

This is probably what it feels like to be dying, she thought to herself, this feeling that I am floating away to somewhere unknown, that my body no longer quite belongs to me. She was conscious of a vague feeling of sadness, but it was a sadness for the grief of her family and friends rather than a sadness for her own fate. My father and mother will miss me, she thought dreamily. She no longer felt cold; just sleepy.

That was a moment of great danger for Nuala. If she had allowed herself to drift off to sleep, she would probably have died. This, in fact, almost happened; but suddenly a thought shot through her mind. There was one creature who had no family and no real friend except herself: Fergus. Without Nuala to love and protect and care for him, he would undoubtedly be killed. By some means or other, she had to stay alive for Fergus's sake.

CHAPTER ELEVEN

In the meantime, Nuala's parents were going through agony. They had not missed their daughter for quite some time after their midday meal. Each had assumed that she was in some other part of the bog. Indeed, the work was so hard that there was no time to stare around, only a continuous bending and half-straightening up and then bending down again.

It was only towards the middle of the afternoon that Niall said, 'Where is Nuala? Why isn't she helping?'

Then Nuala's mother realised that the girl was nowhere to be seen. Even then, there was not much anxiety. Nuala had suffered so much ill-health during her short life that her parents were used to excusing her from much of the hard work which was automatically expected of others.

There was some half-hearted calling, but everyone assumed that she had become tired and had wandered off to gather flowers or to look at birds. It was only when they realised that the fog was growing denser at every minute that their alarm began to grow. The men put down their spades and, straightening their aching backs, joined the others in the search.

In the beginning, there was annoyance in the voices that called, but soon irritation turned to panic. Nuala's mother wandered here and there, tripping on the tough stems of heather, tears running down her face, her voice hoarse and her throat tight. Eva knew quite well the danger that her daughter was in. This was a very ancient bog, and many parts of it had been dug out by people in the past; these sections were full of water, deep enough to drown anyone who fell into them. In the pit of her stomach there was a tight knot of fear as she pictured her beautiful daughter lying dead with her long black hair floating about her.

Hours passed and still they searched. The mist had grown so thick that Nuala's father was afraid that another person could be lost, so he insisted that they hold hands and make a human chain, moving across the bog and shouting as they went.

A terrible conflict was raging in his mind. Nuala was his favourite child, but he had to think of all the family. His wife was at the end of her strength, and he could hear the sharp rasp every time that Finn drew breath. His father was an old man and to stay out any longer might do him great harm, or even kill him. In fact, the whole family would be in great danger if he went on any further. So far, he was fairly sure that he knew the way back to the lane that led to the bog, but if they went any further they might become hopelessly confused – or, worse still, fall into one of the bog pools.

'It's no good,' he said aloud. 'We must go back. I cannot risk the whole family for the sake of one.'

Nuala's mother screamed an anguished protest, but he silenced her with an anger so rough that she hardly recognised him.

'I cannot risk all for one!' he repeated.

They all turned and, wearily stumbling over the rough ground, went back to where the tools and baskets had been left. It was as they were gathering these up that a sound came which turned their blood cold. From the other side of the bog, towards the west, there came a howl, closely followed by another, even more bloodcurdling than the first. The wolves had come.

At that terrible sound, all self-control left Nuala's mother. Her fear of her husband left her as she seized his arm and screamed, 'You cannot leave her here to be eaten by wolves. Cowards! You all go back. I will never leave this bog until I find Nuala.'

She released his arm and turned to go away. Nuala's father was paralysed with anger and shame, but suddenly an idea had come to Niall.

'Mother!' he shouted. 'Don't go away. I know how to find Nuala.'

At these words Nuala's mother stopped and turned. Everyone else gazed at Niall in amazement. He took a deep breath and prayed that the right words would come to him, and that his father would listen to him and do as he said; for suddenly he was quite sure that he did, indeed, know how to find Nuala.

Quickly, and as clearly as he could, Niall told the story of how Nuala had rescued the wolf cub, how she had fed him and trained him, how he could herd cows and sheep and walk among them without even a glance at the animals, how he would obey every order. Last of all, he told how Fergus had been trained to track Nuala and how he never failed to follow in her footsteps, even when the trail had been laid the night before.

When he finished there was a dead silence. Niall held his breath. Eventually his father spoke: 'How can you stop this wolf running away?'

Niall let out his breath in a great sigh of relief. 'That's no problem,' he said happily. 'We made him a collar from an old belt and I can tie a rope around the collar.'

'Go, then,' said his father quietly. 'Take your grandfather back to the fort and fetch the wolf here. It is the last chance.'

'Let me go with Niall also, father,' said Ciaran. 'I will bring back some torches as it will soon be dark.'

So the two boys and the old man set off. The rest of the family settled down to wait, their minds full of fear and anxiety, but with a little spark of hope in their hearts.

Fergus was delighted to see Niall. He had had a long and boring day locked in the cave and was ready for some fun. He was not too sure about Ciaran and growled softly under his breath. Niall checked him sharply and fastened the collar around his neck and tied the rope to it. He wanted to make sure that there was no chance of Fergus running suddenly up to his father and growling at him. It would take some time before his father would lose his hatred and distrust of wolves.

Fergus had been a little puzzled to see Niall without Nuala, but once the collar and rope had been put on him, he knew what was happening. This was the game where he would track Nuala and find her. He hoped she would have his dinner with her, as it seemed a long time since he had been fed by Maeve in the morning.

As the young wolf strode out confidently, tail slightly waving, ears alert and black muzzle testing the air for scent, Ciaran gazed admiringly at the animal. His worries about his sister were beginning to fade with the excitement of owning a wolf. When they reached the lane leading to the bog and Fergus's nose immediately went down to the ground, he realised the truth of Niall's statement. It did, indeed, look possible that Fergus would be able to find Nuala.

Fergus growled again when they came up to the wet and dejected little group waiting at the entrance to the bog. This time, however, it was only Niall, who had his hand on the collar, who heard the growl. Indeed, it was so soft he felt rather than heard it. Obviously Fergus understood that there were more people in his world than he had realised, and that he would have to treat them with the respect that he had for Niall and Maeve. In any case, he was busy casting around trying to distinguish Nuala's scent from all the others.

'Where is Nuala, boy?' whispered Niall. 'Find her then.'

Fergus needed no urging. His nose was to the ground and he ran here and there. The family watched for some time in excitement. Certainly it was easy to see that the wolf was following some trail, but when, for the twentieth time, he came back again to the place where they had eaten their midday meal, hope began to be replaced by the old familiar despair.

Fergus, himself, was puzzled. Usually when he tracked Nuala, hers were the only footsteps and these footsteps went in a straight line. Here, her footsteps seemed to go round and round in circles and were overlaid by so many strange scents that he almost gave up.

However, the most important thing in Fergus's life was Nuala. She was more important to him than food or shelter or even life itself, and he knew he had to find her. Quietly and deliberately, Fergus lifted his nose from the confusing ground and, with Niall in tow behind him, moved up the bank until he reached a higher piece of ground. The fog had thinned out and the west wind from the sea had once again started to blow. Fergus sat down, lifted his head and seemed to smell the wind.

What it was he could smell, the family did not know; but there was no mistaking the renewed confidence with which he got to his feet and began to trot towards the west. After a few minutes he stopped and again put his nose to the ground. The family held its breath, but this time there was no mistake. Fergus was off so fast that Niall could hardly keep up with him. On and on they went across clumps of heather. Occasionally Fergus seemed to overshoot the scent, but each time he quickly realised his mistake and, picking up the trail again, set off with renewed vigour.

Behind them came the family. There was no mistaking the fact that Fergus was definitely tracking something, and a small flame of hope began to flicker in Eva's breast. Her husband also was beginning to hope that he might find his beloved daughter; whether alive or dead he did not dare speculate at this stage.

Mixed in with his hope was a sense of bewilderment. All his life he had hated wolves, trapped and killed them without mercy; and here was one of this hated breed being trusted to find his daughter.

Fergus and Niall had now come to a full stop. Fergus was making strange sounds and Usna was afraid the wolf was about to attack his son. The large intelligent eyes were fixed on the boy's face and strange guttural sounds were coming from his throat. Then, as if despairing of making himself understood, Fergus cautiously climbed over the side of the precipice and once again tried to communicate with Niall. Now the boy understood.

'Father, I am letting go of the rope,' he shouted. 'Fergus wants to climb down here.'

The whole family rushed up to the edge of the precipice. The west wind blowing in their faces suddenly strengthened and blew the last of the heavy mist away. They could see down the cliff side, they could see the uprooted bushes and the overturned stones, and at the bottom they could see the body of the girl, the white face streaked with dark blood and the black hair spread out behind her. No one spoke.

Fergus, however, had no hesitation. Whimpering with eagerness, he slithered down the cliff and bent over Nuala. For one sick moment, Usna imagined that the wolf was about to feed upon the body of his dead child. With an inarticulate cry of rage he scrambled down the cliff, only to stop as the dark eyelashes lifted and the faint voice of his daughter spoke.

'I knew I would see you again, Fergus,' she said, and straightaway fainted again.

CHAPTER TWELVE

There followed weeks of pain for Nuala. She knew that she had a fever and guessed that she was delirious. She must be delirious, because every time she put her hot hand over the edge of the bed, she imagined that she felt Fergus's rough tongue lick it, and she knew that Fergus was in his cave. She tried to summon up the energy to ask Niall about Fergus, but kept sliding back into a feverish dream. She guessed that her uncle who was clever at mending bones must have set and bound her leg, but the pain from it was so intense that she eagerly swallowed the herbal sleep-potions that her mother brewed for her.

Day faded into night and night into day as Nuala lay there, tossing and turning in delirium. But eventually the day arrived when she woke, weak but lucid.

'Fergus,' she said instantly, remembering her strange dreams about him.

'Don't worry about him,' said her mother, who was in her usual place beside her sick daughter's bedside.

'He is with your father,' she continued, laying her hand on Nuala's forehead and noting that the fever had left the girl.

'What!' Nuala sat up in alarm and then lay down again as a twinge of pain shot through her newly-mended leg. 'What is Father doing to him?'

'Don't worry, I tell you,' repeated her mother. 'Ever since that terrible day when Fergus found you lying at the bottom of the precipice, your father thinks the world of him. Fergus is very useful to him, also. This morning he and Niall rounded up the sheep for shearing in the time that it took for the others to find their shearing knives. No one could believe it. Your father tells everyone that Fergus is his new dog.'

Nuala lay back smiling happily to herself. Never in her wildest dreams could she have imagined that things would turn out so well. It sounded as if Fergus was now a member of the family, and a valued one at that.

A few hours later the men and boys returned from the sheep-shearing and Nuala awoke to see, following them in, the handsome young animal who had saved her life. Fergus seemed to have grown in the past few weeks. Nuala's family considered that nothing was too good for him, so he had been fed as much meat as he could hold. Niall had brushed his coat, which was turning a handsome grey, and he wore a heavy leather collar studded with pieces of bronze.

Nuala held out her hand and Fergus swiftly crossed the room and, putting his two front paws on her bed, tenderly licked her pale face.

'I thought that he was going to eat you when he did that the day we found you,' observed her father.

'I never want to think about that day again,' said her mother with a shudder.

'Where did his collar come from?' asked Nuala.

'Your father got it for him at the fair,' replied her mother. 'He sold many cattle and brought goods back for all the family.' She bent down so that Nuala could see the new gold pin which fastened her tunic.

Nuala felt a pang of disappointment; she had missed Lughnasa, the time of the great festival and fair. She could see that Niall had a new musical pipe, and that there was a new spear for Ciaran fastened to the wall next to her father's spear. Every year, her father had got her a present at Lughnasa; this year he had probably been too annoyed with the careless way that she had risked her life and theirs also. 'No,' she thought to herself, 'there will be no gift for me this year.'

Usna could see from his daughter's expressive face the thoughts that were running through her mind. He turned away to hide the smile on his lips and went out of the house and down into the souterrain. The two boys and Fergus followed. While they were out, Eva helped her daughter to put on her best purple robe and brushed the long dark hair until it shone like silk.

'There now, you look like a princess,' she said as she made the girl comfortable at the table.

At that moment Nuala's father came back into the room, closely followed by her brothers. Behind them came Fergus, as before, but this time he was carrying something in his mouth.

'This is something new that he has learned to do,' thought Nuala, but before she could ask any questions, Fergus came over and put the object he was carrying on to her lap. It was a small leather case, carefully stitched. Nuala guessed that her mother had made it. Looking around her, she could tell from the excited atmosphere that there must be something special inside the leather case.

When she opened the case she saw that her present was not just something special but something rich and rare, something which was beyond her wildest dreams. Lying in her hand was an exquisite gold necklace. It was made from two delicate ribbons of gold which were twisted together, with a small loop on one end and a beautifully ornamented hook on the other end. Nuala's mother leaned over and fastened the necklace around her daughter's thin neck.

'I told you that you looked like a princess,' she said softly.

Nuala kissed her mother and her father. Her heart was bursting with happiness and she could hardly express her thanks. Never could she remember being so happy: she was safe and well again, her family loved Fergus almost as much as she did and she had a gold necklace which was more rare and beautiful than any she had ever seen.

It was a pity that the golden moment had to be shattered, but shattered it was, and of course it was Ciaran who had to spoil everything. Nuala was not as fond of Ciaran as she was of Niall. She suspected that he was jealous of her and that he resented the fact that he, who did so much for his father, was not loved by him in the way that Nuala was loved. Now he spoke out harshly:

'After spending all that money on her, Father, it is a pity that you refused the offer that the man from Tullagh made. He offered you three cows if you would agree to let him marry Nuala when she is fourteen years old. If he saw her now, dressed up like a princess, he might offer four cows.'

Nuala stared at her brother in anger.

'It is not true,' she said. 'You are just trying to spoil everything.'

There was a silence. Looking around, she could see from the uncomfortable faces that there was some truth in what Ciaran had said, and her own face grew even whiter. Fergus, sensing her troubled mind, moved closer to her and laid his head on her lap.

'I told you all to say nothing of this,' said Nuala's father grimly. 'You know how ill she has been. Why are you upsetting her like this?'

Ciaran got up and went out quickly. He knew his father's temper and had often felt the weight of his hand.

Usna swore softly to himself as he saw all the bright happiness wiped from his daughter's pale face. He crossed over and sat beside her at the table.

'I have refused that man, Nuala,' he said. 'I have told him that there is no question of arranging a marriage for you at your age. You are still only twelve years old.'

'In any case, he has never even seen you,' said her mother. 'I don't know why he made an offer for you. But now you must forget about all that. We are going to have a special meal tonight to celebrate your recovery.'

The meal that followed was indeed a splendid one. All this time a great haunch of pork had been cooking on the fire and now hot, succulent slices of this were placed on the wooden platters. There was also bread, which was a rarity. Nuala knew how her mother would have spent long hours grinding the corn on her quern, fitting the two stones together, then pouring the grain through a hole in the top stone; next fitting the handle to the hole and endlessly pushing the top stone around, grinding the corn into flour. It was a task which Eva hated as much as her daughter did, and Nuala knew that she should eat some bread to show her appreciation. However, she had little appetite. Round and round in her head went the one thought:

'Was the man from Tullagh that same man that Maeve and I saw that day looking up at the fort?'

During the next few weeks this question stayed in the back of Nuala's mind. However, as the summer wore on and her leg gradually mended, Nuala began to forget her worries. The weather continued to be good. There were very few wet weeks and Nuala was out of doors most of the days. It had been a good year; there were great ricks of hay and of turf ready to be thatched, and in the underground storeroom, far down enough to be safe from rats, there were great barrels full of oats and barley.

September came and still the sun shone. Nuala and Maeve went every day to gather blackberries. These were dried in the sun and packed into smaller barrels to provide fruit for the long winter months. They also gathered hazelnuts from the bushes by the river. Nuala liked gathering the hazelnuts, and she liked putting them in layers into the barrels and sprinkling some sea salt on top of each layer. When she looked around at all the full barrels in the souterrain, she sometimes used to wonder how three families would manage to eat all the food which they had stored. She was old enough, however, to remember the time three years ago when the rain had fallen continually for the whole summer and the hay had become mouldy, and the nuts and fruit had hardly ripened. That winter had been a bad one, even for a rich family like theirs; there had been several deaths from starvation among some of the less fortunate.

Everywhere that Nuala went, Fergus went too. Nuala's mother was pleased about that because, unknown to Usna, Nuala insisted on wearing her gold necklace every day. She wore it tucked into the neck of her tunic, but all the same Eva was afraid that one day someone would see it and try to steal it. Maeve's mother, Orla, was shocked at her friend allowing such foolishness.

'I don't worry about her when Fergus is with her,' said Eva, but she admitted to herself that she could not bear to frustrate Nuala in any wish. Since her daughter's miraculous escape from death, Nuala was, even more than before, the most important thing in her life. The gold necklace set off Nuala's dark beauty so well that her mother could sympathise with her desire to wear it.

Golden September passed and was soon followed by October. Many of the cattle had been slaughtered, and the flesh had been well salted and stored in barrels, but there was still a sizeable herd of over forty beasts. Usna did not often keep so many in the winter months, but this year his crop of hay had been so good that he had enough to feed forty animals in the months when the grass was not so good.

Now that all the autumn work had been finished, Usna, his sons, his brothers and Maeve's father had begun a great task. For many years, Usna had wished for a proper well next to the fort. They did have some drainage wells on the south-eastern side of the fort, but these only filled up during wet weather and they dried out whenever there was no rain for a week or two. All other water had to be carried uphill from the river, and carrying heavy wooden buckets up that steep hillside was a task which no one enjoyed. Usna had great plans for expanding his herd of cattle next summer and, if he did that, he would need a reliable source of water.

The plan, therefore, was to dig a deep well down to the water table and then to dig a shallow, stone-lined cattle drinking spot just next to the well. This drinking place, dug into the clay, would hold water naturally during the winter and during wet weather in the summer. If it did dry up, there would be no problem, as it could easily be filled from the well beside it. Usna decided to dig the well and drinking place on the north side of the fort, as the water would remain cooler and less overgrown with weeds on that side.

Whenever they could, Nuala and Maeve loved to watch the work. The cattle drinking spot had been dug first of all and already it was full of water. During the next few weeks, the work progressed on the well, and after a month it was so deep that the men had to take turns to go down in a bucket. When the person down the well had dug enough earth to fill a bucket, those on top hauled up the bucket and the boys spread the earth over the fields.

It was slow, difficult and dangerous work, but the men seemed to be enjoying it and were cracking jokes and telling stories all the time. Usna was never happier than when he was improving the land in any way, and he knew that this well would be of the greatest use, not only to his own family but to all the families which would come after them.

Every evening they would all sit down to a great meal which had been cooked by the women. The hard work and the days in the open air brought out great appetites and no matter how much food was cooked, it was always finished.

When the meal was over Niall would bring out his pipe and play to them. One evening he played such a sad tune that Fergus put his nose up to the moon overhead and howled dismally. Everyone except Nuala laughed, but Nuala decided that she would teach him how to sing. She herself was a good singer, and she found that if she could hum a particular high note it was usually enough to set Fergus off.

She practised for a few days and then one day, when they were all having a meal together in her grandparents' house, she insisted on bringing Fergus in to sing for everybody. Nuala's grandmother had been terrified of the young wolf until then, but once she heard him sing she laughed so much that she began to lose her fear of him and even to save bones and other scraps for him. Because Fergus had always been fed from Nuala's hand, he took food much more gently than any dog, and soon her grandmother loved him almost as much as Nuala did herself.

One day the two girls and Fergus were standing on the north side of the fort, looking over the wall, watching the men digging the well. Nuala noticed that her father was poking around in the long grass and turning over the heavy clods of clay with his boot.

'What are you looking for?' she asked.

'I lost my knife a few days ago and I just can't find it. I've searched everywhere. I think it must have fallen down the well. I had a last hope that it might be under this pile of clay, but it isn't. I'll get myself a new one when we go to the fair on Samhain. Samhain is only a week away now.'

'Samhain,' said Maeve. 'I had forgotten that it was so near. Are you going to the fair, Nuala? I am.'

Nuala, however, wasn't listening. 'I'll get Fergus to find your knife, Father,' she called down.

'Don't be stupid,' Ciaran sneered. 'How can the dog find the knife? He can't talk, you know. You can't say to him "find the knife" and expect him to understand.'

'Well, he found me, didn't he?' said Nuala hotly.

'More's the pity,' said Ciaran under his breath, but he did not dare say it aloud. His father looked at him suspiciously, but decided to ignore him.

'You can try,' he said to Nuala, 'but don't be disappointed if he doesn't find it. I'm certain now that it is at the bottom of the well. In fact, if he does find it, then you can have the knife for yourself as a present and I will get myself a new one anyway at the fair.'

'Come on, Fergus,' said Nuala, thrilled at the idea of owning a knife. Ciaran was the only one of the family who had a knife. I'll share it with Niall, she decided.

'How are you going to find it?' asked Maeve, as they walked back across the fort towards Nuala's house.

'Well, I think I'll put his old collar on, the one that Niall made for him, and I'll tie the rope on to the collar and then I'll say "find it". I know he is only used to finding people like that, but do you remember last week, when you left your pouch in the long grass? He seemed to smell it from quite a distance, and he walked over and we found him standing over it.'

'I'm sure he will find the knife,' said Maeve happily. She had a great belief in Fergus's cleverness.

'I think we will just walk around all the places that Father goes to,' said Nuala. 'He may not have lost it near the well after all. Anyway, if we go over there now, Ciaran will just keep jeering at us.'

To and fro, backwards and forwards across the fort they went, the two girls following the puzzled Fergus. It was quite a big enclosure and it measured a hundred paces from one edge of the circle to the other, so there was plenty of ground to search. After about ten minutes Fergus picked up something in his mouth and sat in front of Nuala, offering it to her. It was not the knife, but Nuala gave a cry of delight. Last winter her grandmother had lost the brooch pin which held her cloak fastened around her, and now Fergus had found it.

'Oh, Fergus, you are clever,' she said, kissing him and stroking him. 'Wait until Grandmother sees this.'

'Let's show her now,' said Maeve. 'Isn't he clever!' she added, stroking and patting Fergus.

By the time that Nuala's grandmother had exclaimed over the brooch and told Fergus how clever he was, the young wolf knew exactly what he had to do. He had to search any piece of ground shown to him by Nuala. Now he was no longer puzzled. He strode out confidently, his handsome bushy tail waving slightly, and carefully nosed every inch of the ground, patiently pacing up and down.

Eventually, however, they knew that Fergus had searched every inch of the enclosure, and nothing else had been found. Nuala went back to the north wall and called down to her father.

'It isn't up here. Can you think of anywhere else it might be?'

'Well,' said her father doubtfully, 'I suppose it might be in the lane, but it's not likely. I can't think of anywhere likely except around the well, and I have searched every inch of the ground around it, so I know it is not here.'

Nuala and Maeve took Fergus down to the lane and Nuala again said to him 'find it'. Patiently Fergus zigzagged over the lane, testing every clump of grass, but there was nothing there.

'I'm going to take him up near the well,' said Nuala, resolutely. 'That is the most likely place. Father takes off his pouch when he is digging and the knife probably fell out one day.'

Nuala's father was impatient when he saw them start to search. 'I told you I've looked everywhere,' he said, and Nuala saw Ciaran give an unpleasant smile.

'Everyone searched for Grandmother's brooch, too,' she reminded her father, 'and yet Fergus found it after all this time.'

Fergus knew the routine now and went backwards and forwards, not missing a single inch of ground. Suddenly his tail lifted and stiffened. He plunged his black muzzle into a large clump of rushes which grew near to the cattle watering place. He sat down in front of Nuala, carefully holding the little iron knife in his mouth, his large amber eyes glowing with pride.

'Well, I wouldn't have believed it,' said Usna. 'The knife must have been sticking in the ground and the handle was hidden by the rushes. That's why I couldn't find it. He's a marvellous dog. I'll keep my promise to you, Nuala, the knife is yours now.'

Nuala glowed with pleasure.

'Could we take Fergus to the Samhain Fair?' she asked beseechingly. Her father hesitated, but then nodded, and Nuala took Fergus's front paws in her hands and did a little dance of joy.

CHAPTER THIRTEEN

The morning of Samhain, the great feast at the end of autumn, was clear and cold. The leaves had gone from most of the trees by now, but each branch and twig was outlined with little fuzzy spikes of frost. Nuala blew into the cold air and saw her breath rise like a cloud of smoke in front of her. Her hands and face were icy cold, but the rest of her was warm and cosy, tucked in beside her mother on the back seat of the heavy wooden cart, a thick bedcover made from sheepskin stretched over the two of them.

Ciaran and Niall rode ahead of them on their horses, but Fergus trotted beside the cart with an anxious eye on Nuala. This was the first time that he had seen Nuala in the cart and he was worried about her. Soon, however, he relaxed and enjoyed galloping effortlessly alongside.

When they arrived at the fair, however, he was completely bemused. Nothing in his previous life had prepared him for the huge throng of people. Cows and sheep he was used to, but unknown people alarmed him. Glancing at him, Nuala could see that his eyes had become very dark and the hair around his neck was standing up slightly.

'Let me out of the cart,' she said to her father. 'I want to walk with Fergus. I think he is worried by the crowd. I can easily keep up with you. You have to go so slowly now with all the people and the cows and sheep.'

'There's Maeve over there,' said her mother. 'You can join her and walk over with her to the place where the horses and carts are left.'

Fergus was glad when Nuala climbed down and walked beside him. He was now so tall that she could rest her hand on his neck as they walked around, and her touch reassured him. He was delighted to see Maeve amongst all the strangers; his tail wagged and his pink tongue came out and licked her hand.

'Walk on the other side of him, will you,' said Nuala. 'He is worried by all the people.'

They were joined by Nuala's two brothers, who had already tied up their horses. Fergus was now completely relaxed and watched the busy scene with interest. His training had been so thorough that he walked past the flocks of sheep and the herds of cattle without a glance, and soon an admiring crowd gathered around him.

'Is he a wolf?' asked one man eventually. 'He looks like a wolf to me.'

'He's my sister's dog,' said Niall quickly. 'Did you ever see a well-trained wolf like that?'

A few people laughed and the man looked embarrassed, but continued to look at Fergus with great interest. Nuala began to be sorry that she had brought him. There was no doubt that Fergus did look quite different from the ordinary sheepdogs and cattle dogs at the fair.

'Come on,' she said to Maeve in a low voice, 'let's walk over and look at the stalls where the goods are being sold.'

There were mostly women and girls over at the stalls and they did not take much interest in Fergus, although a few of them drew back in alarm when he approached. However, when they saw that he kept close to Nuala and did not look at anyone else, they turned back to examining the stalls. There was plenty for sale. Maeve and Nuala started to look at the necklaces; they had never seen so many necklaces together before. There were necklaces made from glass, necklaces made from bone, from tiny fish teeth, but no gold necklaces. Nuala fingered her own necklace proudly and glanced down to look at it as it lay glinting against the dark purple of her robe.

'I wish I could have a necklace like yours,' said Maeve, looking enviously at Nuala. 'No one here has as good a necklace as that.'

Nuala looked all around. It was true. Not a single woman was wearing as fine a necklace as hers. She smiled with pleasure and then caught her breath with alarm.

'Look over there,' she said in a low voice to Maeve. 'There's that man we saw in the ash tree in our lane.'

Maeve looked and nodded her head. 'It is the same man,' she said in a whisper. 'He is looking at you, too. I think he knows who you are.'

'Let's get away,' said Nuala quickly. 'We'll go and look at the pots.'

To Nuala's relief, the man did not try to follow them over to the stall that sold pots. They spent a long time there, asking the woman questions, while Fergus sat patiently beside Nuala, his head leaning against her leg. He knew that Nuala was uneasy and alarmed, and his eyes searched the crowd carefully for any signs of danger to her.

The woman who sold the pots was very nice and she answered all the questions that Nuala and Maeve put to her. She told the girls that she had come from a long way away, from a place called Loch Gurr, and that her tribe made these pots and sold them at fairs all over the west of Ireland.

'We dig up a big mound of clay,' she explained, 'and we leave it out in the wet and frost for the winter. In the spring we strain anything solid out of the clay, and then we mix powdered crystals with it and let it dry a little. When it is soft, but not too wet, we shape the pots and polish the clay with a smooth pebble from the beach, or with a piece of bone. Then we put them inside a ring of stones and build a big fire over them and bake them until they are hard.'

On the way to the meeting place they met Niall again. He was gazing longingly at a splendid shield made from alder wood and covered with the finest leather. There were all sorts of knives for sale at that stall, also, and Nuala wondered whether her father had bought his new knife yet. She fingered her pouch, where the knife that Fergus had found was lying, safely tucked into a little leather sheath which her mother had stitched for her.

Maeve's mother and father were by the cart when eventually the girls found it, and the two families had their midday meal together. Nuala and Maeve told about the friendly woman with the pots and Nuala's father showed off his new knife proudly. Its blade was made of iron, just like the one that he had lost, but the hilt was of a strange metal, much whiter than iron.

'That's silver,' explained her father. 'It comes from under the rocks in the Aillwee mountains over there. They dig it out and melt it and pour it into a mould to set, and while it is still soft they can carve these patterns on it.'

When the meal was over and everything was packed away in the carts, plans were made for the afternoon. The two men and Nuala's brothers went off to watch the horse racing. Nuala and Maeve decided to listen to the storyteller, and their mothers went happily off to shop for new pots and a couple of new pails made from alder wood. It had been a good year for the cattle and they were able to get goods in exchange.

After a while, Nuala and Maeve got tired of the storyteller. They had heard his tale before.

'He says it all too quickly, anyway,' said Nuala. 'He is only showing off what a good memory he has. My grandfather tells that story about Queen Maeve and the Cattle Raid much better. He makes it sound really exciting.'

After leaving the storyteller, they lingered for a while listening to a horn-player. Then they joined a crowd who were watching two men playing at dice, tossing up the small cube-shaped pieces of bone and deftly catching them in mid-air and slapping them down on the flat piece of stone.

It was while they were standing there that Nuala felt the hair on Fergus's neck began to rise. She looked quickly down at him and saw that he had his eyes fixed on a pair of large hounds that were standing beside a man. The dogs were very large, even bigger than Fergus, with broad muscular chests, and they were both growling ferociously. The man looked at them in alarm. He spoke to the dogs sharply.

'Get down,' he said. To Nuala he added, 'Don't worry, they never fight. They are very well trained.'

He was wrong, however. No sooner were the words out of his mouth than the two dogs sprang across and hurled themselves at Fergus, biting at the thick hair around his neck. Fergus whipped around and tried to shake the dogs loose, but he could do little as they held him firmly from both sides. He was bleeding now; Nuala could see the red stain spreading on the grey fur. She screamed. Her three brothers came running up, but no one dared to intervene in the terrible fight. The owner of the hounds ran around shouting ineffectual commands, but they were deaf to their master's voice.

It seemed as if Fergus was being brought to the ground by the weight of the two hounds. His head sank down and his legs bent. Nuala screamed in agony, but Fergus recovered his footing and managed to get his teeth into one of the hounds. He was now fighting back, and if he had had only one of them to deal with, it might have been an equal fight; but no sooner did he engage with one hound than the other attacked him from the opposite side, so that Fergus was continually whirling from one to the other.

'Get my father, quickly!' said Nuala to Maeve, and Maeve darted away through the crowd.

'They've got him by the throat,' shouted one of the onlookers. 'It's all over with the grey dog now.'

The owner of the hounds made one last, desperate effort. Seizing the top hound by his tail, he pulled with all his strength and managed to get him off Fergus. But the other hound had the soft flesh around Fergus's throat in his mouth and nothing could shift him. Fergus was tiring and he had almost stopped struggling.

Nuala knew that she had to do something quickly. She took from her pouch the little iron knife which

her father had given her, and before anyone realised what she was doing she darted forward and quickly thrust the tip of the knife into the hound's mouth, right between his teeth. With all her strength she twisted the knife and felt the teeth open slightly. That momentary loosening of the grip was enough, and in a second the owner had managed to drag the second hound off Fergus and to slip the leash onto him.

At that moment Nuala's mother and father arrived and found that the fight was over. Nuala was on the ground beside Fergus, who was drawing in great sobbing breaths of air. Nuala's father dropped to his knees beside Fergus and parted the thick grey fur on the throat and examined him carefully.

'He'll be all right,' he said eventually. 'It's just a bad bite. It will heal up. His fur saved him. Another inch and he would have been dead.'

The hounds' owner came up to them, shocked and upset.

'I am very sorry,' he said. 'I don't know what got into them. They have never fought before. I think it must be because your dog looks a little like a wolf and they are bred to kill wolves.'

'Well, yes,' said Nuala's father thoughtfully, 'he does look a little like a wolf, I suppose. It must be the colour of the fur. Still, there's no harm done. We'll put some comfrey on it tonight and he will be right as rain in a few days. See, he's getting to his feet already.'

After this no one wanted to stay any longer, and they got on the cart. Fergus was hoisted up by Niall and Ciaran and lay comfortably with his head on Nuala's lap. He was beginning to recover his strength, but the nearer he was to Nuala, the happier he felt.

CHAPTER FOURTEEN

Twice a day for the next week, Nuala and her mother
put a poultice of well-soaked comfrey leaves on the
wound on Fergus's neck. Nuala tied some strips of
linen around the comfrey to keep it in place. In the
beginning Fergus tried to tear off the dressing. But
Nuala spoke sternly to him and he lay down by the
fire, staring miserably into it and hating this wet,
strange-smelling mess clinging to the fur of his neck.
Nuala sat on the floor beside him, stroking his head,
and that made it more bearable for him.

'He won't need to keep it on all the time,' said her
mother, looking sympathetically at Fergus's
depressed face. 'If he hates it too much, you could take
it off after a while.'

'No, it'll be best if he gets used to it,' said Nuala
firmly. 'I want him to get well quickly. I don't want
to run any more risks with him.'

After three days of this treatment, the wound on
Fergus's neck was almost better.

'I think you could leave off the dressing now,'
observed Usna, examining him carefully. 'He's a
young dog and his flesh is healing very fast. The air
will do it good.'

'Oh, good,' said Nuala happily. 'I got such a fright.
I thought those two hounds had killed him.'

'They nearly did,' said her father dryly. 'I don't
think you should ever take him to a fair again. Those
hounds were really only doing what they have been

bred for, and that is killing wolves. No matter how much we tell people that he is a big dog, the hounds will always know that he is really a wolf.'

Nuala nodded. 'I know,' she said. 'I made up my mind to that when we were coming home from the fair. Really I was only taking him because I was so proud of him. I don't think he liked it much. He is much happier around our own land, and when he is happy, I am happy.'

There was one thing, though, that Nuala was unhappy about at this most happy time of her life, and that was her father's order that Fergus had to be chained up with a great iron chain every night. Nuala knew that Fergus would have liked to sleep on the ground beside her bed, and she had begged and pleaded for this. Her father, however, stood firm.

'Look, Nuala,' he said, 'if anyone around here has a sheep or a cow killed during the night, they might think that Fergus had done it. If we can say that he is chained up every night then no one can accuse him.'

Nuala, however, still hankered for Fergus to stay with her at night; and there came a time when Usna wished that he had given in to his daughter.

It had been a fine, frosty day at the end of January. The family had gone early to bed, worn out with the preparations for tomorrow's festival of Imbolc, the festival dedicated to the goddess Brigit. Fergus, as usual, was chained to the post at the entrance to the fort. Niall had made a little house for him, filled with rushes and covered over with the old sheepskin which Nuala had used for him in his cave. It was warm and cosy and usually Fergus slept happily there.

Tonight, however, he was uneasy. He sat up very straight and turned his head slightly to one side, listening intently. No human ears could have heard the sound, but the sharp senses of a wolf picked up the faint murmur of human voices. A slight north-westerly wind began to blow, and now Fergus was quite sure that something was amiss.

It is a strange thing: human sweat can betray fear to almost every animal, but much more to a highly intelligent alert animal like a wolf. And if that wolf has had his intelligence deepened and sharpened by contact with man, then his powers are all the greater. Fergus could smell fear and treachery in the air.

He was still a very young animal, only just over a year old, and in the normal pack situation he would have kept very quiet and left the elders of the pack to make the first move. However, after about five minutes had passed, Fergus became uneasy. No one in the fort had moved, but from outside he could hear the stealthy sound of men moving about and, more ominous still, the heavy hooves of the cattle. Some people, not belonging to Fergus's family, were driving the cattle away.

As soon as Fergus realised what was happening he lifted his nose to the sky and began to howl. In the beginning there were sleepy shouts of protest from the houses and Niall was sent out to quieten him, but Fergus continued to howl and the forty cattle added their voices to his.

Now everyone realised what was happening. They rushed out of the houses, snatching spears and stones as they set out in pursuit of the cattle thieves. In the excitement, no one thought to release Fergus, and he continued to howl and to strain against the heavy iron chain which was tied to his collar.

Usna, his brothers and his sons were fleet runners and even old Finn, spurred on by anger, was going as fast as he could. All the cattle had been in the Big Meadow, a few hundred yards from the north-west side of the fort. The cattle thieves had, in addition, had a good five minutes' start.

A few clouds had blown across the sky and the night was pitch black. Usna could see nothing, but he could clearly hear the cattle in the distance. They were all protesting loudly and their hooves were thundering on the heavy ground. The strangers no longer had any reason to keep quiet and their shouts and curses filled the air, as did the sound of heavy blows across the backs of the unfortunate animals. Usna swore. Almost the entire herd was in calf and even if he got his cows back, treatment like this could cause the loss of many calves. The thought lent him fresh energy and he spurted ahead, overtaking Ciaran who had been in the lead.

Suddenly the clouds cleared and the full moon shone out, lighting up everything, and Usna could quite clearly see the cattle thieves. They were quite near, and, judging by the sound of their breathing, they were badly winded.

Usna stopped behind a thick hedge and the others stopped with him. Taking careful and deliberate aim, they hurled their iron-tipped spears at the raiders. A scream of agony came from one man and a grunt of pain from another as two of the spears found their mark. The other two men hurled their spears, but Usna and his family had ducked down behind the hedge, so the spears went wide of their mark.

Snatching up the two spears, Usna and his brother Conor advanced on the men, followed by the rest of their clan.

It never even looked like being a battle; two of the men were wounded and the other two were disarmed. In a few minutes all four were lying on the ground, securely bound with leather belts. Usna interrogated them while his sons rounded up the frightened cattle.

'Where do you come from?' he asked sternly.

'From Tullagh,' answered one of the men sullenly.

'Why do men from Tullagh come to rob me of my cattle?'

'It was not our fault,' said one of the wounded men resentfully. 'It was Brian, our chief. He was angry because you refused to let him marry your daughter Nuala when she is old enough.'

Usna's face grew dark with anger. 'And where is this brave Brian, then, that he may make his complaint to my face?'

The men looked at each other, but made no reply. An icy fear gripped Usna's heart. 'Where is he?' he cried again.

Slowly and reluctantly one of the men answered: 'He stayed behind at the fort. He is going to steal your daughter.'

While all this was going on, Nuala and her mother sat huddled together in front of the fire in the little house. They were almost paralysed with fear. This was the first time that there had been a cattle raid at their fort, but they had heard terrible tales of the bloody battles which sometimes occurred. Cattle were the most important goods for the people in this part of the country, and there were many who would kill in order to build up a large herd.

Their terror was made worse by the unearthly howling that still came from Fergus. He seemed, as the time went on, to be making more noise rather than less, and Nuala could hear the clank of the chain as he desperately strove to be free.

'Why didn't Father take him?' wondered Nuala. 'Fergus would have been of more use to him than Niall or Grandfather.'

At that moment came an agonised screaming howl from Fergus. Nuala got to her feet, determined to go out to him. She crossed the flagstoned floor, pushed aside the heavy sheepskin which hung in front of the entrance and stepped out into the night.

At that minute the moon came out from behind the ragged clouds and Nuala gave a gasp of horror. Standing in front of her was a small, dark man whose greedy eyes were fastened on the gold necklace around her neck. It was the man from Tullagh.

Nuala's heart began to pound so fast that she could hardly breathe. Before she could cry out, a hard hand was placed across her mouth and nose, and the man from Tullagh began to drag her, not towards the entrance where Fergus was howling and straining at his chain, but towards the north side of the fort.

Normally, there was a high wall all around the fort and a deep ditch beyond, but during the work on the well, that wall had been breached on the north side and four tree trunks had been placed across the ditch. Obviously, the man from Tullagh had come in that way. He would never have got past Fergus if he had come through the normal entrance on the east side. Now he was going to drag Nuala through that same way, and there was nothing that the securely-chained Fergus could do to help her.

In the midst of her terror, Nuala was conscious of a feeling of overwhelming rage. As hard as she could, she bit the hand over her mouth. The man gasped in pain and slightly withdrew his hand. Nuala screamed and kicked him as hard as she could.

The man seized her by the hair with his free hand, grasping the gold necklace and jerking it so that the scream was suddenly cut off in her throat and she felt as if she were being slowly throttled. Realising that she would soon lose consciousness, she fought with all her might, squirming this way and that, trying to break the man's hold. However, there is very little that a twelve-year-old girl can do against the strength of a man used to hard physical work, and inexorably he dragged her though the hole in the wall of the fort.

It was at this moment that everything changed. For the last few minutes Nuala had been aware, in the back of her mind, that the howling from Fergus had stopped. Now she knew why. With a flash of white teeth and a ferocious growl, the young wolf hurled himself on top of the man's chest. The gold necklace snapped, and with a despairing yell the man overbalanced and fell into the newly-dug well.

Minutes later, Usna struggled up the hill, sick with apprehension, to find a white-faced, shaking girl staring down at the dark surface of the well. The great silver circle of the moon was reflected in the black water, but no sign of life stirred its still waters.

The body of the man from Tullagh was recovered from the well the next day, but Nuala's necklace was not found. Nuala mourned her necklace very bitterly, but in the end she accepted that it would never be found.

She was wrong. It was to be found, but only after many hundreds of years had passed. And that is another story.

FAST-WING

Séan Kenny

'Have you seen any other Ducks like me?'

When a young Blue-Winged Teal is blown off course in a storm, he finds himself in a strange land. Nobody has seen a bird like Fast-Wing before, and not everyone likes him.

Is he really a bad omen for the birds of CourtMac Bay, as the powerful Black-Back Gull claims? Will he ever find his flock again?

An inspiring story of friendship, courage and leadership as the young bird triumphs over loneliness and exile.

Fast-Wing *is a tale that will remain with readers long after they reach the final page.*

ISBN 0-86327-547-8

RUN TO THE WILD WOOD

Tom McCaughren

The gripping new wildlife adventure from the award-winning author of *Run with the Wind*; *Run to Earth*; *Run Swift, Run Free*; and *Run to the Ark*.

When man destroys the badgers' home in the Fragrant Wood, they turn to the foxes for help. Old Sage Brush gathers a group of foxes to lead the badgers to a new home. Young Scat is thrilled to be included in the group – but he knows, from their friend Ratwiddle's strange predictions, that some of the foxes may not survive the journey. The Giant Hounds are soon hot on their trail – and who knows what other dangers lie in wait for them on their quest for the Valley of the Dragon?

'Entertainment and suspense at its best, it is the Watership Down *of the fox world...You could almost believe that Tom McCaughren has some magical way of making himself small and invisible, so that he can live among the foxes whose lives he describes so well.'*
Irish Times

ISBN 0-86327-492-7

ELSIE AND THE SEAL BOY

Patrick O'Sullivan

Some say that the story of the boy brought up by the seals is only a legend – but as Elsie is drawn into a mysterious water-world, she discovers the wonderful truth...

A suspense-filled, magical tale from the bestselling author of *A Girl and a Dolphin*.

ISBN 0-86327-558-3

Available from book shops or direct from
WOLFHOUND PRESS
68 Mountjoy Square
Dublin 1
Tel (01) 8740354